DRAGON'S JINN

Dragon Point Eight

EVE LANGLAIS

Copyright © 2021, Eve Langlais

Cover Art by Yocla Designs © 2021

Produced in Canada

Published by Eve Langlais

http://www.EveLanglais.com

Digital ISBN: 978 177384 223 3

Print ISBN: 978 177384 224 0

All Rights Reserved

Dragon's Jinn is a work of fiction and the characters, events and dialogue found within the story are of the author's imagination and are not to be construed as real. Any resemblance to actual events or persons, either living or deceased, is completely coincidental.

No part of this book may be reproduced or shared in any form or by any means, electronic or mechanical, including but not limited to digital copying, file sharing, audio recording, email and printing without permission in writing from the author.

Prologue

Maalik had his first vision of the future at the age of three. Leftover lamb stew for dinner again. Yuck. It also happened to be the same day he discovered he could change the course of what lay ahead, in this case, by tipping the pot and ruining the meal, which led to him also learning that altering upcoming events could have consequences. It took days for the pain in his buttocks to subside.

It wasn't the last glimpse of the future he would have, nor the last time he would act to interfere. Some things were easier to manipulate than others.

Ensuring his mother would say yes to a request or that a certain girl would smile a certain way? Easy. Getting the boys to not punch him for being strange? Not as simple. Until he came into his true power as a mage.

As one of the elite, he was accorded advantages but also great responsibility. Especially since he could see what was yet to come. In order to counter a world that literally erupted into flames of destruction, he aligned with the most potent dragon mages of their time—which included him.

Together they sought to rid the world of an invasion by a race most commonly known as the Jinn, smoky spirits that could grant wishes to those that captured them. Small things for the most part, until the Jinn began to merge. Apparently, the smoky spirits fractured when crossing into the dragon's world. Once they melded together, they became new entities, powerful ones that called themselves the Shaitan. Their sole goal was to bring the Iblis, a big bad monster, into their world from another dimension.

The dragon mages swore to stop it, mostly because Maalik told them if they didn't, all life would cease to exist. He'd had a vision, rife with death and violence. A planet ravaged by war. Ruined unless he and twelve others made the ultimate sacrifice.

Their lives in exchange for a chance to end the evil threat once and for all.

Young heroes will always be brash and agree until reality sets in. In this case, to save a future still far away, a spell was cast. It sucked the thirteen dragon mages into a cavern system that sat outside of time. A place of no escape and the most meager chance of survival, where thirteen best friends eventually turned on each other. Where love splintered. Hope shattered. And all because Maalik sought to change a future he didn't like.

Three thousand years later, the door to their prison opened. Four of them left the moment they could. Their arrival didn't go unnoticed by a vastly changed world that had ceded magic for technology.

The modern era—which was very concerned about categorizing things—had a name for the four mages. Apparently, scriptures spoke of the four horsemen of the apocalypse. What the stories didn't impart was they didn't just herald the end of times. With the arrival of the dragon mages, magic was fully breathed back into the world.

What no one knew? Those four weren't the only survivors. While the harbingers of the end of times sought out the artifacts imprisoning the Shaitan, one dragon mage had a quest of his own to fulfill.

Long after Azrael, Nikhail, Jeebrelle, and Israfil emerged from the sand, a fifth followed, his robe dusty, his staff gnarled and old like him. The cowl was deep enough to hide Maalik's grim expression. Determined, his eyes perhaps a little wild in his zeal. Time to make a wrong, right.

And have another chance at love.

Chapter One

"Poor guy honestly believes he's got it all worked out. But you know what they say about the best-laid plans. They end up not having butterscotch ice cream for their apple pie." Elspeth, a cheerful, if crazy dragon, uttered the nonsense out of the blue.

Like, seriously, the woman had appeared out of nowhere and started up a conversation as if they'd been strolling together all along.

Babette "Babs" Silvergrace looked around, but sure enough, they were the only two around. "What are you talking about?"

Sometimes talking to Elspeth could pose a challenge. She saw things about people and the future. Those around her, friends and family, learned a while ago that ignoring her wasn't an option.

"You haven't met him yet. But you will. Soon. First, he's got something to do. And so do you." More cryptic nonsense.

Having ridden this coaster before, Babette rolled with it. "Will I have fun?"

"Don't you always?" Elspeth countered.

"Will I get to hit something?"

"Is that even a question?" Elspeth had gotten better with her sarcasm.

"This thing I'm going to do, is it the king sanctioning it?" Not that it would matter. If Elspeth said jump, Babette leaped to the sky.

"The king will approve once he hears of it. He's rather distracted right now."

Understatement. Of late, their newly anointed dragon king had not been commanding much, as everyone waited for his mate to give birth to the heir. A baby who would hopefully take after their golden father, a wise and firm leader.

Or would the child be more like its uncle, the first dragon mage in centuries?

Speaking of whom, a glance at the field showed Samael sparring with magic against Azrael, one of the four horsemen of the apocalypse and a dragon mage from a time before the ban on magic when their kind ruled. Azrael and the others recently released had brought arrogance to a new level.

Babette admired their disdain so much. Especially since they didn't hold back—*Did hot water make you soft? Perhaps you'd like your mother to squat over you for a few more years while you mature.* Add in the fact that Azrael had agreed to teach Samael how to use his power and you were talking pure entertainment.

"I'll wager two of my pumpkin spice Twinkies Azrael flattens him," was Babs' gleeful prediction. She should have known better than to wager against their resident psychic.

Elspeth smiled. "Sure."

Babette grimaced even as she asked, "What are you wagering if I win?"

"My first-born child."

And with that, Babette knew she'd lost because if there was something Elspeth would never give away, it was the baby growing inside her. Anyone who even tried to lay a hand on the child would have to deal with her husband, Luc, the overprotective demon from another dimension. While Babs didn't see him in the vicinity, she had no doubt he was nearby. The man obsessed over the safety of his wife, and with good reason. With Elspeth off the drugs to keep her from seeing, the visions sometimes took her and wrung her out hard, leaving her pale and shaking, sometimes foaming at the mouth.

Before Babette got to know Elspeth, she hated

her cheerful attitude about everything until she grasped it was the only way for the woman to handle the shit her mind made her see.

Sure enough, Azrael didn't even dodge the fireball Samael tossed. He flicked his hand and scattered it into harmless sparks.

Appearing bored, Azrael drawled, "Are you ever going to try, or shall we end this now with you dunked in the pond again?"

The vein in Samael s forehead throbbed, but that was the only sign of his agitation. He'd gotten better at controlling his temper, and his magic had improved obviously, given he shrugged, as if conceding, just as he hit Azrael with a bolt of lightning!

It knocked the dragon mage down, and Babette held her breath. Would the older mage kill Samael?

Azrael popped up and grinned. "Much better. Again."

Samael nodded, and they went back to the insults and magic.

Elspeth placed her hand on Babette's arm. "You have a visitor."

The announcement caused Babette's heart to race because there was only one person she ever wanted to see these days. "Where?"

"The usual spot." A statement that cemented it.

With unseemly haste, Babette bolted for the garden, a maze of hedges modeled after the one in *The Shining*. The twists and turns to reach the bower took too long, even as she didn't hesitate once in her path. She emerged not quite panting but definitely looking a bit too eager. No one was there.

Good. She took a moment to compose herself. Never look too eager. She lounged on the stone bench, the picture of nonchalance for when Jeebrelle arrived.

Babette greeted her with a smile. "Hey, Jeebs, imagine seeing you again."

The horsewoman of the apocalypse, dressed in a light, frothy, pale cream-and-green-hued dress, cocked her head. "Really? Because the odd one told me you were waiting for me here."

Bloody Elspeth. Bless her heart. "So what brings you?" Please let it be a sign Jeebrelle was interested. From the moment she'd met Jeebrelle, she'd wanted to lick her head to toe and lots in between. Unfortunately, Jeebs had yet to give a sign she was into Babs. Or girls for that matter. Yet, she had hope, given Jeebs kept seeking her out specifically.

"I need your help."

"Sure!" Oops. A little too eager.

Still, she didn't regret it once Jeebrelle smiled. "I was hoping you would agree."

"Agree to what exactly?" Not that it mattered. She'd do anything Jeebs asked, short of killing her family. Although there were a few cousins…

"I require your aid in tracking down one of my brethren." Jeebrelle clasped her hands.

"Which one?" Obviously not Azrael since he was lobbing balls of ice at Samael, who deflected with an air shield. That left the one with mangy cat—Israfil—and the fourth one, Nikhail, whom she'd not really gotten a chance to meet yet.

"We must find Maalik. One of the thirteen."

The name brought a frown. "I thought only four of you survived that time loop spell?"

"We thought him dead. However, recent events have shown that to not be entirely accurate."

"Wait, so there's five horsemen of the apocalypse? Because the stories only ever talk about four." And boy were they wrong. Not only was one of them a girl—and the hottest thing since that ghost pepper sauce Uncle Manuel made—they were dragon mages and one sorceress. Which Babette found much sexier than the term mage.

It made her wonder if Jeebs had a sexy outfit to use for doing magic. Because nothing screamed practical like a skimpy bikini. Easier for shifting in.

Rowr.

Jeebs's lips flattened. "The legends of this time are fanciful fluff with hardly any basis in truth. We are hardly the bringers of the apocalypse. We are here to stop it. And the reason we're here is Maalik. He's the one who trapped us for three thousand years. The one who lied an unseemly amount. He has much to answer for."

"Would you like me to hold him down while you purple-nurple him?"

That made the other woman blink. "Is it painful?"

"Very," Babette stated with a nod of her head.

"Then yes, we shall purple his nurples." Jeebs bit her lower lip. "Perhaps you can show me how it's done?"

She had to swallow hard just to squeak, "Okay."

"Excellent. We really mustn't let Maalik keep the artifact for long. Who knows what kind of trouble he can cause if he lets loose the Shaitan in the ring he absconded with."

"Does it really matter if he lets the genie go? If it causes trouble, then we'll just poke it with the God Spear." A cool weapon made out of dracinore coveted by all the dragons since its recent elevation from ordinary to magical monster killer. Azrael currently had possession of it. None had stolen or challenged him for it, but there was talk, especially by those who possessed hoards of weapons.

"It is not the Shaitan being loose I'm worried about but what Maalik might wish for," Jeebrelle muttered, the fabric of her dress swirling in agitation.

"So long as it's not the end of the world, does it really matter?" Wishes had limits apparently. Little things, like a new wardrobe or a freezer full of ice cream, easy to do. But ask for some really big stuff—like world peace or a moon really made of cheese—and the magic collapsed and weird shit could happen.

"That's the problem. What Maalik wants, he can never have. Magic can't bring back those that are lost."

It took a second to filter. "Wait, he wants to wish someone back to life?"

"Yes."

"Zombies. Cool." She'd have to brush up on her movies.

"It doesn't happen."

"Not true. I've seen your horses. They're dead." And like solid ghosts when they appeared, which made no sense.

"Because we bonded their spirits to the remains of their flesh. It can't be done with dragons."

"That you know of," Babette added because she liked to be a shit.

Jeebs shook her head. "Even if it were possible, and Maalik wished Ellona back to life, he won't get what he wants." Jeebrelle's expression turned sad. "Have you ever loved someone who just doesn't love you back?"

"More times than I can count." Babs fell in love quickly. She was the first to admit it. Problem being, most of the time, that love was bad for her.

But there was always the next time.

"Where do we need to go to find him?"

"I thought perhaps we should start with his last home."

"Wouldn't it be gone?" Because short of a few Aztec ruins and Middle Eastern structures, very little survived that length of time.

Jeebs rolled her shoulders. "It could be his cave has been destroyed, but it's a start."

"A cave?" Her expression brightened. "What's a dragon mage cave like? Will it have magical traps? Some cool robes? Pointed hats? Should I bring a whip?"

"Knowing Maalik, nothing that interesting."

"What's he like?"

"Serious. Seeing the future took its toll on him, as did the promise he extracted from us. I'm afraid we didn't react kindly. Then the loss of Ellona…" Jeebrelle's voice trailed off. "He's not in his right mind. You'll help me find him?"

"Anything. I'm all yours." And she meant that quite literally.

Chapter Two

The ring Maalik stole, not long ago during a rooftop gathering of dragons, glinted in his grip. It was a vessel for a Shaitan. One of the seven seals holding back the Iblis, a force that, if unleashed, would destroy all life.

Breaking the artifact and freeing the Shaitan shouldn't release the Iblis, not with four more seals remaining. Even if it accidentally happened, they now had a weapon against the Shaitan. The newly created God Spear that could actually destroy them rather than scattering them into smaller pieces that were less powerful but still pesky.

Maalik hesitated. Since he'd filched the ring from under his brethrens' noses, he'd pondered the wisdom of using it.

It had taken the efforts of many dragon mages to trap the seven Shaitan in the first place. Some of mages died. Thirteen more went into a place where time didn't affect them, not physically at least. Emotionally, it took its toll. Imagine having nothing but time on your hands.

Maalik managed to replay hundreds, thousands of moments in his life, every mistake to figure out where he'd gone wrong. So many ways he'd erred. What if he could fix the most grievous one? Return to an era gone by and make a different choice.

The ring sitting in the palm of his hand dared him. Not the most ostentatious of artifacts. A thick gold band, rife with symbols whose meaning had been lost to time, unless you were one of the original thirteen. Three thousand years hadn't been long enough for him to forget the language only known by dragon mages.

It had been long enough for him to regret, though.

Maalik bore the full brunt of responsibility for them being imprisoned for too many lifetimes in a network of caves. At the time, because of his visions, he'd thought it provided the only way to save the world. They would be the shield against the Shaitan when they were released. It would have been better if they could have killed them. If they'd only had a way.

It took a human, *a simple human*, to figure out how to defeat the enemy. A woman of less than half a century—now mated to his brother Azrael—accidentally released a Shaitan and made a wish.

People often made the mistake of generalizing their demands, making their wishes impossible to accomplish. Had Daphne, the human in question, said, "*I wish the Shaitan could die by being stabbed with a fork,*" it would have failed because there were protections within the wishing magic for that kind of broad, generalized request. But this human, who had only recently discovered a world beyond her imagination, had used her wits to tailor her demand.

"*I wish that, from this day forth, the stave that Azrael currently wields be known as the God Killer, the one weapon that can destroy any sentient being in this Earthly dimension.*" The elegance of her demand kept the magic focused and doable. Despite the wish being deadly to the Shaitan who granted the power, bound by their own rules, they couldn't stop it.

And so, three thousand years after the wars, with lives ruined and lost, they finally had a way to fight. One of the Shaitan had been removed from existence. The others were scattered and appeared to be trying to stay hidden.

Good.

If the Shaitan weren't scheming, then the mages didn't have to worry about them finding a way to open an inter-dimensional portal. The Iblis, their master, would remain locked in its prison. The world was safe. Breaking the ring and freeing one more Shaitan wouldn't change that fact, but Maalik would be granted three wishes.

Only three to make things right.

The ring taunted him.

Let me loose, and I will give you everything your heart desires.

At what cost? Because it might have taken thousands of years, but Maalik finally understood all magic, especially deep desires, came with a price.

Would it be too high?

Maalik couldn't see his own future, and for three thousand years, he'd slept and not dreamed. Since his return, his visions had resumed, but most were mired in a fog that wouldn't let him see much but chaotic glimpses that made no sense. Israfil's ugly cat, an eagle, a flying horse, the seas turning red…

What if, in his ignorance, he managed to ruin

the current peaceful balance? Doing nothing, though, wouldn't ease the gnawing guilt within.

He held up the circlet. He'd come this far. Hidden from his brethren. Lied, and now stolen. Would he really let doubt guide him now?

Resolution firmed his grip around the ring. He had a plan, and it was good. He'd spent a long time perfecting it in his mind. It just needed one final step.

Destroy the ring, free its Jinn, making it beholden. What better place to destroy metal than a forge?

The one he'd located didn't look anything like the ones of old. For one, it resided within a city in the basement of a building a few stories high. Something they called a converted warehouse. The heat remained the same, though. The moment he'd stepped into the forge, the blast of hot air hit him, and for a moment, he closed his eyes and remembered his home. He'd yet to return and see if his cave had survived the eons. Maybe once he'd redeemed himself.

A burly fellow with a bushy beard and goggles pushed up on his head turned at his entrance. "Who are you? What are you doing here?"

Did this human truly question him? The nerve.

He'd not once seen a future where dragon mages would be so disrespected. "You are hungry. You will go get some food and not return for at least an hour." Maalik pushed the suggestion at the man, using magic.

"I am starving," the fellow declared and departed without a backward glance. Humans were so easy to convince.

The man's removal left Maalik alone with the forge that was hot enough to melt metal.

He removed the ring from his pocket, and he stared at it. Was he really going to destroy it? He still remembered the battle to capture this one. A Shaitan with feminine curves wrapped in veils of smoke. Her laughter was deep and rich. Her smoky touch left behind pleasurable shivers.

He remembered wavering in his resolve. She'd not been as bad as the others when it came to causing trouble in the world. But she was still Shaitan. One of the Iblis servants vowing to release the menace. And now he would release her.

He reminded himself he would control her.

Control it. Best to not think of it in personable terms. It was a monster that he would use.

Three wishes and he already knew the first one.

Pinching the ring, he extended it over the fire.

"Don't you dare!" growled a familiar voice.

But hearing it wasn't what stunned Maalik. Blame the fist, a real one with knuckles and force, behind the punch out of nowhere that dragged him into the past.

Chapter Three

The vision struck Maalik after their final battle. His knees hit the ground hard, not that he noticed. He'd fallen into the future, a strange one with mysteriously tall and gleaming buildings. Metal chariots that had no animals pulling them raced along stone roads packed with traffic.

He saw a time when the seven seals they'd struggled to create were located and their dangerous entities released. A world where the Iblis came through a dimensional rip and destroyed all life.

It left him shaking. Not just with disbelief but anger. They'd fought hard to contain the threat. Surely their efforts weren't in vain?

He pounded the ground with his fists. How do I stop this possibility?

Maalik couldn't always control what he saw, but this time, with the hard ground grinding into his knees, his mouth *sour with the sickness brought by his sight, his power showed him a way.*

No.

What he saw...it was too much to ask. Anyone who agreed would be condemning themselves. And yet, try as he might, he saw no other path.

Thirteen dragon mages would have to give up their lives that a handful of them might stop the coming apocalypse. Wiping his mouth, he dragged his feet returning to his brethren.

He could hear their boisterous voices as they teased, thinking their hard work done.

Azrael held a bag in his hand. Within was an artifact with the last Shaitan they'd captured. "Now that they're trapped, hopefully things can go back to normal."

"Drinking, wenching, and doing very stupid things." *Ridwan, a lifter of skirts and yet surprisingly free of bastards, grinned.*

"The stupidest," *Nikail agreed. His expression sobered.* "I can't believe we did it." *He probably wished they'd been successful earlier given what it cost him. A mother. A sister.*

"Don't celebrate yet." *Maalik joined them, shaky within but knowing he had to speak now while the adrenaline coursed through his friends.*

"Why not? Once this is buried and forgotten"—*Ridwan pointed to the bag*—"it's done. No more Shaitan, no more Iblis. We won."

Azrael must have seen something in Maalik's face because his expression fell.

Maalik's stomach churned, but he knew he had to tell them. "It is only a temporary victory. The Shaitan will return."

"A problem for another generation," Ridwan declared. "We did our part. Saved the world."

"You only delayed the inevitable. Those prisons won't hold them for forever. I saw it. Saw what happens when they return. Rivers of blood. Screams of the innocent." Maalik found himself falling into that cesspool and would have been sick again if his body had anything left.

"How long before the Shaitan escape?" Ridwan asked.

"Not for a while," Maalik admitted. A very long while, but it would happen.

"Meaning we might be long gone. Someone else will have to fight them," Nikail pointed out.

Maalik shook his head. "The generation that will eventually face the Shaitan will fail. They won't have magic."

"How can they have no magic?" Azrael exclaimed. Theirs was a time full of portents and power.

"The world moves on. Some things go extinct. When the Shaitan return, no one will know how to stop them."

"Meaning the Iblis will come." Nikail ducked his head. "All we've done is for nothing. We've only delayed the destruction."

"There is a way to ensure that doesn't happen." Maalik

wanted to scream at the unfairness. Hadn't they done enough?

"You've got a plan?" Azrael was never one to shy from danger.

Maalik nodded. "There is a way to ensure there are people to fight the Shaitan and teach a future generation how to use magic. All we have to do is bind ourselves to the spell holding the Shaitan in their prisons." He made it sound simple.

It wasn't.

"Bind ourselves how?" asked Ridwan.

"With magic. My vision showed me how." It had also showed him that not all of them would survive. However, he kept that part to himself lest they fail before they begin.

"Wouldn't it have been more useful for your vision to show you how to kill the Shaitan rather than trap them?" was Ridwan's complaint. "Why can't we rid ourselves of them now while we have them contained?" He grabbed the chainmail sack and shook it.

He had a point, but one problem remained. "I don't know how to get rid of them. All I know is that I've seen the future where we're not there to fight them. Maybe you can live the rest of your life knowing the world is doomed, but I can't," Maalik snapped.

Ridwan sighed. "I hate it when you make me want to be noble."

"How long are we talking?" Azrael asked. *Because it obviously wouldn't happen in a natural lifetime.*

"A timeframe wasn't clear." Did his friends hear the lie? Because, while Maalik couldn't give an exact count of years, he knew it was a long time. Longer than any of them could imagine.

Azrael bowed his head. "Whatever it takes."

Ridwan and Nikail readily volunteered, barely waiting a beat before declaring they were in.

Grief threatened to close his throat. "I knew I could count on you." Maalik knew before he asked. Knew how he could use their honor against them.

But they were only a handful. He needed more.

That night, as he prepared for the celebration marking their triumph in trapping the seven Shaitan, the magnitude of what he'd condemned his friends—and those he still had to convince—to, sent him back to the ground, head hanging. Weak with guilt. Sick with it. Angry, too. Why was it up to him?

Ellona entered his chamber and exclaimed seeing him on his knees. "Maalik! What are you doing? The feasting has begun."

"I know." He'd smelled the roasting of meat since his return to the village, and his mouth watered. But knowing what he must do next? It killed his hunger.

Her gaze turned soft. "You saw something." A friend since they were hatchlings, Ellona knew about his power, even encouraged it. She brushed his cheek. "Surely it can't be that bad."

How he loved her, which was why he had to spare her. "I need to go away for a while."

"Where are we going?"

We. Because they'd been a team since the beginning of the Shaitan threat. Lovers, too.

"You can't come," *he declared even as he wanted nothing more than to bring her on this next journey.*

Her hand dropped, and she frowned. "Can't? Why not?"

Because it would be selfish to take her knowing she might not survive. "This is a journey for others."

Her expression hardened. "Who else is going?"

"I don't know yet. It's not entirely clear." *The future had granted him the choice in that at least. In his vision, he'd seen only shadowy shapes, thirteen in total, standing in a circle with Maalik at the center. Which of them made it to the future? Which of them would die because of the choices he made today?*

"You're not going anywhere without me," *was her obstinate reply.*

"No!" *he shouted at her.*

"You don't want me with you?" *In that moment, Ellona's vulnerability shone through. Everyone knew her as a warrior mage. She often led the charges in battle. Fearless in the face of adversity. But with Maalik, she showed a softer side.*

"Of course, I want you with me. It's just... This will be a trial unlike any we've faced so far."

Head tilted, she stared him in the eye. "Then we will surmount it together."

She had no idea what she promised. He did, and yet he still accepted. "Together."

In that moment he damned them both.

As Maalik roused from the past, he could hear Israfil haranguing. "Don't you pretend that little tap hurt. Open your eyes, dammit. Face me!"

Maalik's lashes fluttered, and it took a moment for his vision to clear. He blinked, but what he saw didn't change.

The incongruity wasn't of Israfil holding Maalik by the shirt and shaking him but of the slick feline perched on Israfil's shoulder.

"Is that a cat?" Not hello or sorry for imprisoning you for three thousand years, how's it going? He was curious about the critter holding on to his enormous friend.

"Aha! You are awake," Israfil announced.

"You have a cat?" he couldn't help but question because Israfil wasn't the type to own a pet. And Maalik hadn't ever *seen* it either.

"Don't change the subject. What is wrong with you?"

"Many things apparently," was his dry reply.

Including the fact he no longer had the ring. Damn Israfil for taking it while he was knocked out.

Still holding him by the shirt, Israfil glared. "Let's start with the fact you're alive."

"You don't say. How did you find me?"

"Not easily, you bastard." Israfil punched and then dropped Maalik, who rolled before rising.

Maalik wiped at the blood streaming from his broken nose. "Feel better?"

"For now. I might change my mind later," Israfil grumbled. "You've much to answer for, starting with, how is it you're not dead? Azrael said you jumped in a lake and never came back out."

"I went somewhere." Looking for a person and a thing. He found neither.

Israfil snorted. "Obviously. And now you've returned, apparently with your own agenda. Again." His gaze narrowed. "How much of what you told us was a lie?"

"Technically, none of it."

"Omitted, then," Israfil growled.

"A few details, perhaps."

"Three thousand years," Israfil rumbled. "And you bring us back to save a world overrun with humans."

Maalik hung his head. "I didn't see—"

"You overstated the issue to get us to play along with your hero complex."

Maalik gaped. "My what?"

"You, always claiming a need to save the world. Turns out the world can save itself just fine."

"I was trying to help."

"Harrumph." A disgusted sound rather than a fist. "I take it you're going to claim stealing this ring is to help the future."

"Not exactly," he hedged.

"You're going to have to do better than that. You stole it. Why?" Israfil crossed his arms, while his cat sat and stared. An incongruous pair.

"You two will be together a long time," he predicted.

The cat yawned.

Israfil made another noise of irritation. "Stop changing the subject. Why did you take the ring?"

"Why does it matter? It's not as if you'll give it back," Maalik complained.

Israfil stared without blinking, as did his cat. "I don't have it."

"What? If you don't have it, and I don't…" Their gazes swiveled to the dirty floor underfoot.

"Did you hear it fall?" Maalik asked.

"No. I was too busy keeping you from falling face first into the fire."

"Thanks. But that wouldn't have been an issue if you'd not hit me." The complaining was familiar. How long since he'd argued with his friend?

"I couldn't help myself. Your face was too tempting a target."

"We need to find that ring." Or all Maalik's plotting would be for naught.

The feline jumped to the ground. They searched even as Maalik kept casting stray glances at the forge. Had he dropped the ring into it?

If so, where was the smoke? The vengeful Shaitan?

As they searched on hands and knees under tables and stools, Israfil grumbled, "Why did you steal the ring, anyhow?"

"I needed it for something."

Israfil paused in his search. "Only one thing to do with it. You wanted the wishes."

"Maybe."

"Don't maybe me," Israfil roared, diving for him. "I can't believe you wanted to release a Shaitan."

Maalik rolled and dodged his friend's—ahem, current enemy's—hands. "With one Shaitan already dead, the Iblis is contained. It won't matter if I release it."

"Are you stupid? Shaitan are dangerous."

"I have a plan." Spoken just as Israfil managed to grab hold.

Israfil shook his head. "I know what you're thinking. You can't wish her back."

"I'm aware. But…" Maalik paused. "I wanted to try and make things right."

At the pathetic words, Israfil released him. "And how did you figure a wish would help? Ellona's dead, Maal. You have to move on."

His shoulders lifted and dropped. "I've tried. I just can't. It's my fault she's gone." His fault he was miserable.

"And what did you think releasing the Shaitan would do? Were you going to wish her back to life? We both know there is no magic strong enough to do that."

"Not entirely true. It just takes the right sacrifice."

Israfil blinked at him. "You'd give your life?"

"I'd give anything if I could wish the woman I love back into existence."

"Your wish is my command, Master," said a husky voice, and a naked female stepped out of the forge.

Chapter Four
_____

Despite being newly released, the Jinn noticed Maalik's and Israfil's shocked looks. They were her sworn enemies. She should smite them. Bring down this building on their heads. Call up a swarm of insects to sting them. Give their man parts a terrible itch.

However, the Jinn was distracted by her body.

She poked it. She had an actual body made of flesh. Odd and a first for her. Usually, her smoky presence could only give a semblance of being solid, and just for a few moments at a time unless tethered to the material plane.

The men argued.

"...can't believe you released a Shaitan."

"You hit me. This is your fault," declared the seer.

"Don't you blame me. You should have seen this was going to happen," Israfil bellowed.

"Meow."

Ignoring the males, the Jinn crouched to better see the cat that cocked its head at her. She stared into its wise eyes. "You've been touched by them." Them being the others of her kind.

Her kind? Since when did she view herself in the singular? Since when was she a she?

The snapping of fingers drew her attention to the males now fixated on her rather than each other.

"Are you the Shaitan from the ring?" the one known as Maalik asked.

"Yes, Master." The link between them, created because he was the last to hold her prison before her release, had her using the honorific.

A new master. *Ugh.* Her nose wrinkled. Another new thing. How fascinating. She poked at the tip of it. Felt it and scrunched it. Not only did it act like a real nose, she could smell, too. It wasn't pleasant.

She opened her mouth. *Ew.* She could taste it. Before she could wish away the nastiness, fingers snapped. "Pay attention, Shaitan."

She focused on Maalik with his hair drawn back showing off his mighty scowl. "Is the master ready for his second wish?"

"*Second?*" The word was echoed by both males.

"What was the first?" Israfil asked.

"To bring the women he"—she pointed to Maalik—"loves into existence."

The seer arched a brow. "Which has obviously failed seeing as how Ellona isn't here."

The rebuke brought a frown, and a strange feeling of confusion. "Who is Ellona?"

"The woman I love. Have loved for three thousand years."

"Whom you should have let go a long time ago given what happened," Israfil muttered.

"I know not who this is Ellona is, only that I've granted your wish."

"Says you. Show me where she is." Bulky arms crossed over his chest.

Did he think to bully her? That wasn't how wishes worked. "Would you like to make showing her your second wish?"

"No, I want proof I got the first one. Where is Ellona?"

"Somewhere, I imagine." The Jinn waved her hand.

"Alive?"

"Maybe."

"What do you mean maybe?" he yelled. "Did you or did you not bring her back to life?" He huffed, his eyes blazing with wrath. It was attractive, which in itself was odd because she'd never noticed beauty or ugliness before.

"You didn't ask for this Ellona's life. You asked me to bring back the woman you loved. Your wish was granted. Whether it's to your satisfaction or not isn't part of the deal."

"How do I know you gave me what I wanted?"

She rolled her shoulders because it felt appropriate. "Because that's how the magic works. Would the master like to make another wish? Perhaps for a nicer demeanor? You're handsome, but your attitude is unattractive."

"This isn't funny." He ground his teeth and growled. "I want to know what you did with my first one. Which, I will add, wasn't an actual wish. I didn't know you were released and was speaking hyperbolically to my friend."

"It counts. Do you think you're the first to try and argue that?" She smirked. "It might have been three thousand years since I last had to grant one, but I remember the rules. You made a wish. I granted it. You have two left. Choose wisely. Personally, I'd think about asking for a fresh wardrobe."

"You're one to talk."

She glanced down at her body. "Why ruin perfection with fabric?"

His nostrils flared as he stared at her face, then lower, then back to her face. "Put some clothes on while I think."

"Is that a wish, Master?" She said it on purpose to annoy and felt a satisfaction when Maalik's jaw tightened.

"No, it's not. It's called decency."

"But I'm not decent," she teased. This was probably the longest she'd ever chatted with a dragon mage. Usually, they were about trapping her or slicing her into tiny bits.

"I can't believe you released a Shaitan." Israfil looked on with disapproval. "I'll call Azrael and have him bring the stave."

At that statement, Maalik stepped in front of her as if to protect. "No. You can't kill her. Not yet."

The very idea. She laughed. "Mortal weapons can't kill me."

"Think again," Israfil announced. "A human wished for a way to conquer any living entity. There are now only six Shaitan in the world."

"That would explain the disturbance I felt," she murmured aloud. Also, quite frightening. A Shaitan never died. They could be broken into smaller pieces, but eradication? Unheard of until now and a frightening prospect, given she'd only just escaped her prison. An unjust punishment at that.

"Think you can hold her in place while I fetch Azrael? Better yet, you fetch him while I watch her." Israfil scowled in her direction.

"No one is killing her," Maalik argued.

"What he said." She couldn't believe she agreed with her enemy.

"The Shaitan is dangerous," Israfil countered.

"I agree, and once I get my wishes, you can do whatever you like."

"Objection!" She raised her hand, not understanding the gesture.

They spoke as if she hadn't.

"You know the others won't be happy about this. Wishes are dangerous."

"Which is why I've crafted the perfect ones." Maalik eyed her for a second before returning his attention to his friend.

"Perfect? Doubtful. We both know they'll twist your demands."

"Hence why the need for careful choosing of words to impart only one intent."

"Tell me," Israfil said. "Let me be the judge of that."

"I can't. She ruined my first one, which means they need to be reworked." Maalik's brow creased.

Israfil sighed. "Maal—"

He interrupted. "I know you think me insane. I swear I know what I'm doing."

"Said by every person who made a stupid wish." She grinned. "So go ahead. Let's see if you can do better than them."

Her words clearly discomfited both men. Good.

"Can't you see? They want you to do this." Israfil gestured in her direction.

Maalik wouldn't be dissuaded. "Give me a few days. A week at most. I promise I won't ask for anything that will cause harm to anyone."

"Except yourself," Israfil grumbled.

"After what I did, do you really care?"

"Surprisingly, more than I thought I would." Rubbing his hair, Israfil groaned. "Fine. A week. But then, no matter where you are, I will find you and end the threat myself."

"See you soon," she said with a wave and a giggle. He'd find her not that easy to get rid of. They might have stuck her in a ring for who knew how long, but she'd escaped and didn't plan on being captured again.

Israfil whistled. The cat leapt to his arms then clambered to his shoulder. He called a portal and left.

She turned a smile on Maalik. A warmth filled

her as she looked on him. A strange feeling that had her jutting a hip and offering him a smile. "We are alone now, Master. What can I do for you?"

It had an effect. Maalik's nostrils flared, and his eyes lit.

Having seen lust before, she recognized it and took a step toward him. This would be easier than expected.

"What are you doing?" he snapped.

"Me? Nothing."

"Stay where you are."

"Why?"

"Because." His fists clenched by his sides.

She ignored him and moved until she stood close enough to scent him. Feel the heat of his fleshly form. Sway toward him. What strangeness imbued her, as if taken by a spell?

Her head tilted. His angled.

Their lips drew close, and she wondered if they would embrace in the manner humans did to show carnal affection.

Instead of a kiss, he whispered, "We have to leave before my brother returns to kill you."

"He said you have a week."

"He was lying. I've seen a future where he returns with the magicked stave and kills you where you stand."

Her eyes widened. "Where should we go to be safe, Master?"

"I don't know. This world is so different. Nothing is familiar. I need somewhere I can think."

"Fear not, Master. I know just the place." She clapped her hands and *poof*!

Chapter Five

One minute they were in the forge, and the next, a dusty cave.

Maalik's cave, as a matter of fact. It was still intact after all this time. Just as empty, too. Unlike his brethren, he'd not started a hoard in his youth. A part of him always knew he'd have to leave it behind. Was it strange to regret not having done the things others his age had? He'd never been one to wench or covet. He'd not basked in the glory of a collection but rather roiled and fretted about the way the future kept shifting no matter the tweaks he made.

In the end, all of his worry had no effect and his visions failed him. A human was the one to solve their Shaitan problem. Those three thousand years of isolation for twelve good people—and one well-meaning seer—proved unnecessary. Actually, it might have been detrimental, given how, later on, dragon mages were banished to another dimension.

Perhaps had they remained they'd have made a difference?

Maybe he and Ellona would have lived happily, ruling their chunk of the kingdom. Except, even before the decision he'd made, he'd never seen a future where Ellona ended up married to him.

So he chose a way to bring them together. Every day. Without respite. Who knew that would begin to grate so early in their confinement?

"This is not very grand," was the announcement that dragged him back to the present. It drew his gaze to the Shaitan, who looked nothing like the evil smoke he remembered battling.

She remained naked. Very womanly. Her shape curvier than Ellona's athletic build. Her hair, the deep dark of midnight, fell down her back and hovered around her hips. As she moved, her buttocks peeked through, slivers of firm smooth flesh. When she whirled, the strands of silk parted in sections to show off pert breasts with large, dark nipples—and no navel!

Because she was Shaitan. A medley of Jinn. Not dragon. Nor even part human.

The reminder killed his ardor and soured his

words. "What would you know about a home? The Shaitan don't have any."

She arched a dark brow. "Who told you that?"

He opened his mouth and shut it. "I just assumed."

"Not entirely wrong. I had a home. It's gone now."

"How do you know? You haven't left my side."

Her lips twitched. "I meant the one I left behind to come here to this world. I'd yet to establish a proper one before my unjust incarceration."

"Hardly unjust," he muttered.

"Matter of opinion, wouldn't you say?" Her voice lilted.

"How did you know this was my cave?" Back in the day, he'd kept it well hidden.

"I know many things. Ask me a question."

"And lose another wish? No thank you. Just like you'd better not count this as a wish. I never asked to come here. You did this on your own."

"You said you needed a place to think. I'd assumed your home would be a peaceful locale to do so. I see I might have been wrong." She grimaced as she looked around. Small channels in the rock filtered the barest of sunlight into the space. "I thought all dragons lived in wondrous places."

Shame proved hard to quell. "It's been three thousand years."

She made a deliberate show of examining the room. "I'd say it hasn't changed much since then."

The embarrassing truth had him rolling his shoulders. "I had bigger things to occupy my time, like saving the world."

"And how did that work out for you?"

"I saved it, didn't I?" Spoken sourly. Had his choice even made a difference, or would the events have still transpired if he'd never cast that damnable spell?

"Congratulations. Here's your ribbon." She handed him a silky blue strip that said, "Participant."

He slapped it to the side. "This isn't amusing."

"I agree. You don't seem happy. Why is that?" she pointedly asked.

His lips pressed tight. "None of your business."

But did the woman listen?

She tapped her lower lip. "I'll bet this has to do with this Ellona person. Did you have to leave her behind when you imprisoned yourself and your friends?"

"I didn't imprison us. I ensured we'd be around when the Shaitan threat returned."

"Is that how you sold it to your friends?"

His jaw shifted. "I didn't know it would be for that long."

"But you did know they'd be awake and aware, that it would last a long while, and that the world they emerged to wouldn't be the same as the one they left."

Each statement hit him like a barb that tunneled into flesh.

He held himself rigid lest he squirm. "Our sacrifice wasn't in vain. The world is safe, and those that survived may now live as they want."

"And yet here we are."

"I didn't say mistakes weren't made along the way."

"Which you want to fix using magic." She smirked. "Thousands of years and nothing has changed."

"What's that supposed to mean?"

For just a second her countenance turned sad. "As if you don't know. You're just like the rest of the people in this world. Using us for their own selfish needs."

He wanted to refute her claim and couldn't. He frowned. "If you don't like doing wishes, then why do the Jinn offer them?"

"Because of the bargain."

"What bargain?"

"The Jinn are not from this world. We fled ours because of a great danger. But it came at a cost. The guardian of this place bound us with a promise. It seemed simple enough. If captured, then whoever frees us shall receive three wishes."

"With caveats."

"Of course, there are limitations, or with the very first wish, we'd have died. We always give exactly what is asked for if it is within our means."

"But it often doesn't match intent."

"And how is that our fault?" She moved away, the sway of her hair hypnotic.

How long since he'd noticed a woman? Too long if he found himself eyeing the enemy with anything but hatred.

"How is it you have a body?" he asked. He'd never known the Shaitan or lesser Jinn to be anything other than smoke that, even when solid, had a spongy feel to it, as if you could plunge a hand in and have it emerge out the other side without hitting anything.

She glanced down. "I am not sure how this occurred, only that your request triggered the flesh."

That brought a frown. "I didn't wish for you to have a body."

"No, you didn't," she agreed but said nothing more.

"If your body is a result of my wish, then you obviously erred because I most certainly did not ask for that. Meaning, you still owe me three wishes."

For a moment, she stared off, eyes unfocused before shrugging. "Nope. You still only have two."

"That's not fair." He clenched his fists, hating the whine in his tone.

"Don't get angry with me. It is not I keeping score but the bargain that binds me."

Her use of singular pronouns struck him. "You keep speaking in the first person. I thought the Shaitan acted as a collective."

"We do. I did." Her forehead creased. "It is most odd, but since my return, I am very much aware of myself. In that I have thoughts and feelings that appear to be my own. Something I've not experienced before. I can only assume that my long imprisonment is to blame."

"So you're not sharing thoughts with the other Shaitan?"

"No. My mind only holds me, and my actions are my choice." She sounded rather adamant about it.

"Says you."

"I have no reason to lie."

"Nor a reason to tell the truth either," Maalik countered.

A smile tugged her lips. "Correct."

"This world you fled, what was wrong with it? Did the Iblis destroy it?"

She shook her head. "Nothing of the sort. Our sun was dying. It was leave or die when it went out. The Jinn who could, fled."

"And now you want to help the Iblis come across!" He spoke bluntly.

"Actually, no."

Her reply startled him. "What?"

"While some of the Jinn have fallen for the Iblis's pretty promises, there are those of us who know that its brand of destruction won't stop at humans and other creatures. Humans and dragons aren't the only ones with a sense of mortality."

"If the Shaitan know it will eventually turn on them, then why?"

"Some of them are just that dumb."

"And you weren't? I thought you shared thoughts."

"It's complicated," she advised.

He scrubbed a hand through his hair. "You're lying. I saw it. You want to free the Iblis."

"Did you really see that?"

"In a few futures."

"And did those futures show the fact you pushed the Jinn to the extreme?"

"Don't blame us for your actions."

"Yet, it is your unwelcoming antics that led to the Jinn uniting. We were being harmed. We reacted."

"Harmed how?" he scoffed. "You're smoke."

"You think when you chop us into small pieces it doesn't hurt?" A technique they'd used to weaken the Shaitan because, when reduced in size, they weren't as powerful.

For a moment, guilt filled him. It had never occurred to him it might actually cause them pain. Or he knew but didn't care because the Shaitan were monsters. Hard to remember that fact when he stood talking to one.

He changed the subject. "How many Jinn does it take to make a Shaitan?"

"One."

"I don't understand. I know you can be broken into pieces." That remained capable of giving wishes, just much weaker. Ifrit, the even more fractured kind, couldn't do much more than blow lightly.

"Pieces that are still part of a whole. Over time, they reassemble. It is the Jinn way."

"And it hurts?"

She cocked her head. "Not in the physical sense you're implying. When pieces of me are apart, I am less. My sense of me is weak. But once I am whole again, I am more for the shared experiences while we are apart."

He blinked. "Well, fuck." Probably the only modern word that could truly and eloquently express his feelings.

"Given your quest to eradicate my people, I'm surprised you know so little about us."

"I—"

She interrupted. "Made assumptions about our intentions."

"Did I? Because I still remember whole villages dead by Jinn magic."

"You punished an entire species for the crimes of a few."

"I did it to save—"

"You did it because, like many young males of your time, you wanted someone to fight because staying at home to be an overlord for farmers, whose sole purpose was to stud and get fat, was boring."

Sounded like his father. A man who probably died bloated from eating sheep, while drinking wine and fornicating. The only good thing about that was the man only fathered a few bastards.

"I would have welcomed peace," Maalik claimed.

"Liar. We both know you could have enjoyed a lifetime of peace and died of old age in bed. Admit it, you saw a future where treaties among our kind would make fighting obsolete."

"A few, but most promised death and destruction."

"And fighting appealed to you because you wanted to make your mark. Perhaps to impress a girl."

It would be dishonest for him to ignore the fact that Ellona played a part in his decisions. Ellona had always been drawn to more dangerous elements. Given a choice, Ellona always wanted to fight. And he wanted Ellona.

It wasn't as if he exaggerated the danger the Jinn posed. It wasn't hard given the disasters posed by some of the wishes, because people made the mistake of thinking they could ask for anything.

I want to be rich.

Someone died, and they inherited.

I want someone to love me.

That kind of forced affection never ended well. By the third wish, things got really ugly.

It was so easy to convince people like Ellona that they could be heroes. The adrenaline of the chase left them flushed and arrogant. It also led to passion. Going after the Jinn resulted in Maalik getting the girl he'd always wanted.

She'd followed him into that cursed place. Found out that their love didn't do well without strife. So they fought. A lot. Because of him, Ellona lost her chance for a happy life of her own.

He eyed the Shaitan and her dangerous speaking of the truth. "You're right. I could have chosen a different way. But I didn't. And there isn't a day I don't regret my choice."

"You admit your mistake?" Her mouth rounded in surprise.

"I've had a while to think upon it."

Her expression turned sly. "Why not wish it away?"

"Because we both know that's too big of a wish."

"It would depend on how you phrased the scope."

"Hypothetically, what would happen if I asked to return to a specific spot in time?"

"Travel to the past isn't possible."

"Because you're too weak."

"Because of the paradox created."

"Then I guess there is no way for me atone for my errors in judgment."

"There is still a way."

"How?" he growled, moving close to her. Enough she had to tilt her head to meet his gaze.

"I'm sure you've thought of it. After all, you said you regretted your actions. So why not end everyone's misery?" She suddenly held up a vial. "This will help you get rid of that pain."

By the smirk on her lips, he understood what she implied. Maalik grabbed her by the arms and growled, "I am not going to commit suicide."

"Is that a wish?"

He shook her. "Cease speaking."

"Or what, *Master?*" she mocked.

Before he could reply, someone interrupted with a cheerful, "You might want to unhand the little lady before I remove those hands permanently for you."

Chapter Six
_____

A few moments earlier...
"You sure this is the place?" Babette asked, glancing around.

They were in the middle of no-fuck-land where the air was so dry she felt her pores squeezing shut, trying to preserve what little moisture she had left, which was none. She'd sweated it out about ten miles ago after she and Jeebrelle emerged from the portal. Jeebrelle had mis-recalled the location of Maalik's cave, so they walked through the middle of nowhere, desiccating with every step.

Jeebrelle waved a hand. "Maalik was never one for fancy accoutrements. Then again, why bother when he knew what would happen to us?"

"How did he know?" she asked, wondering if them talking aloud would alert the man. Yet, try as she might, she couldn't speak directly to Jeebs's mind.

"Maalik is a seer."

"Really? Can he predict who will win the Super Bowl or the next stock that will go viral and make big money with little investment?" Because Babette's luck hadn't gone well so far.

"Perhaps. Maalik can't always control what he sees."

"But he saw a need for you to get locked up for an eternity."

"At the time, he told us he didn't know how long it would be. Had I known, I wouldn't have spent so much time and attention on collecting dates."

Babette arched a brow. "Dates? As in people or the fruit?"

"Fruit. I find them to be delicious."

"And not that rare anymore."

"Neither are your cakes with the frosting in the middle." Jeebrelle had been one of the lucky few invited to visit Babette's hoard. If only Babette hadn't been too uncharacteristically shy to find out if Jeebs might want to be lain down on a bed of cakes and thoroughly enjoyed.

"Guess we both have a thing for sticky stuff that requires licking." Babette winked, and no mistaking the spot of color in Jeebs's cheeks.

She wore yet another lovely dress that would make access to her treasure so easy. The dragon mage halted their climb of a hill to declare, "We're here."

Babette glanced around. The spot was pretty much the same as all others. "Here where? Because I don't see our boy."

"Boy?" Jeebs snorted. "He's older than your family combined."

"But obviously acting like a teenager with a hard-on given he stole a magic ring to bring his dead girlfriend back to life." Which was the condensed story Jeebs gave Babs.

Jeebrelle's lips flattened into a thin line. "That is only a hypothesis. I could be wrong. And in any matter, he shouldn't be playing with wishes. Not after everything we did to trap the Shaitan in the first place."

"Then let's go get him. I assume he's somehow inside the hill you made us climb?"

"It used to be a mountain," Jeebs muttered.

The sand and dirt had piled against it over the centuries and taken away that lofty title.

"I don't suppose there's a door?" Babette asked because the stony ridge they stood on certainly didn't offer one. Not even a crack.

"Through here." Jeebs walked into the rock.

Literally.

Babette stared. She'd not seen a shimmer as if it were a mirage. A press of her hand showed it solid. "Um, Jeebs? I don't have that kind of magic." Not the kind that let her walk through stone at any rate.

Rather than receive a reply, a hand reached out and grabbed Babette's wrist. With a hard yank, it pulled her through. Her gasp cut was short by a hand over her mouth.

Which she obviously tongued. Jeebs's turn to suck in a breath.

Unfortunately, before Babette could really impress with her oral skills, Jeebs removed her hand and whispered, "He's here." She then pointed, and Babette noticed they stood high up on a ledge, looking down into a deep cavern lit only by a few orbs strung around. Enough to show two people standing at the bottom.

A far bottom. Good thing she could fly, or she'd worry about turning into a meat pancake if she fell off the ledge. As the bigger shape grabbed and shook the smaller one, all thoughts of flirting vanished—until later. Hunter mode kicked in, and with a swagger she'd earned, Babette took the lead. In a low drawl, she said, "Stay behind. I'll handle this."

She leaped from the ledge, the whistle of the

desert wind in the cracks hiding the noise of her descent. Neither the man nor woman was alerted to her approach, but that could be blamed on the arguing.

Babs might have listened more if not distracted by the naked boobies on the female. Nice breasts that went with a hot body. It led to Babette being a tad protective when the dude shook her.

Being chivalrous, Babs threatened to remove said hand if he didn't release the naked woman at once.

Not the best of greetings, but it did not deserve the reaction she received, as the big man suddenly went dragon, of the most impressive size, and boomed inside her head:

"WHO DARES ENTER?"

Chapter Seven

The sudden intrusion by the woman was almost as interesting as Maalik in dragon form. He did it in the blink of an eye, literally. He emerged big and of a strange hue that one moment appeared to shimmer opalescent to purple to obsidian. He also possessed intricate curling horns, a sign among his kind that he had magic.

And he used it, grabbing the intruder and stringing her up by the ankles.

Not that the woman cared. She laughed. "Dude, what did your mother feed you? You are absolutely massive."

The dragon grumbled.

He went still as yet another woman appeared, drifting down in a frothy mess of fabric, the gown the palest green hinting of yellow. Her hair was bound atop her head in intricate braids that the Jinn wondered at now that she had strands of her own. The slender female wore gloves over her hands, hiding those deadly fingers.

This was the plague mage, Jeebrelle. Deadly when it came to humans and their frail constitutions, merely annoying to the Jinn, whose smoky presence tended to not attract viruses.

"Calm yourself, Maalik. It is only I."

That didn't seem to reassure him, for he shuffled in place, his massive dragon bulk brushing against a cavern wall, sending dust and loose fragments down.

"Don't you dare act annoyed! If anyone has the right, it's me, making me think you were dead," chided the plague mage while shaking a finger in his direction.

It fascinated to see the massive dragon hang his head.

"Ah, he's like a sad puppy. Can we keep him, Jeebs? I promise to feed him and take him for walks." The dangling woman's jesting brought a roar, and Jeebrelle laughed.

"Babette! Now is not the time. Maalik is not the type to enjoy casual jesting."

"So he's one of those boring mages. Ugh. Maybe you should let him keep the ring and wish for someone to get the stick out of his dragon butt."

Maalik bugled his annoyance, while the Jinn bit her lower lip because it was rather amusing for some reason.

As for Jeebrelle, she sighed. "Alas, that stick goes too far, so no point in trying."

The dragon huffed hotly.

"Don't be difficult. You know why I'm here. Hand it over." Jeebrelle held out her hand.

The dragon glanced everywhere but at the extended limb.

Jeebrelle frowned. "What's that supposed to mean?"

"I think that's a no," Babette offered.

"More like he can't," the Jinn explained.

"Can't?" Jeebrelle's gaze swung her way.

"He doesn't have it anymore."

"Then who does?"

"No one. It's gone. For good." She might have been a tad too gleeful about it, but three thousand years stuck inside? She had reason.

As Jeebrelle cocked her head, the writhing tendrils that had escaped her braid stilled. Her big eyes became dark as the pupils widened. Her red lips parted, and she whispered, "Maalik, what did you do?"

The dragon whined like a dog who'd done wrong and pissed in his master's boots—because a certain captive Jinn offered him a treat if he did.

The plague mage planted her hands on her hips. "Don't you start with your attitude. I will have answers."

"And maybe ask him to let me down. Gently," the upside-down woman suggested.

"Put Babette down at once. And then change into a shape where we can all converse because I don't get the impression your guest can hear us."

As heads swiveled to eye her, the Jinn grinned. "Plague mage. Long time no see."

Jeebrelle's lips pursed. "It is you. I wasn't sure given you're not usually that real looking. Been practicing your shapeshifting skills while inside the ring?"

"I had the longest nap actually. And then my master released me and gave me flesh." Not exactly a lie.

Jeebrelle gaped. "He did what?"

"It's not like she's making it out to be." Maalik returned to being a man, fully clothed since a mage of his talent had no issues with that kind of simple trick. "I accidentally made a wish, and the Shaitan became flesh. Or so she claims." He glowered in her direction.

She smiled and waved.

"How do you accidentally…? No." Jeebrelle shook her head. "I don't want to know. But I will say, what is wrong with you? I thought we were supposed to prevent the seals from breaking, not destroy them ourselves."

"I have a plan."

"A plan even better than locking us up for a few thousand years?" Jeebrelle asked sweetly.

"Oooh, you're in trouble," Babette crooned, actually orating the Jinn's own thought.

"I'm going to make things right," Maalik declared.

"Unless you're planning to rewind time and never trap us, I don't see how." Jeebrelle glanced over at her. "Can you rewind time?"

She nodded. "Yes."

"You told me no!" Maalik interjected.

"Because it is both yes and no. The issue with time travel is if you change anything that affects the future where I do send you back then you create a paradox where I never sent you, thus it didn't happen and well…"

"But it can be done," Maalik insisted.

"Not in a way that you could survive. Don't you think if we could travel back, we would have already done so? Or do you think we enjoyed our time in captivity?" She couldn't stop the sarcasm.

"You weren't supposed to enjoy it. You were imprisoned for being a menace."

"A menace?" She laughed. "We aren't the ones who started the war. We came here simply wanting to exist, and then, when it was discovered we had magic, everyone wanted to use us."

"Don't play as if you were the victim. You wanted to bring the Iblis here knowing he'd destroy everything." Maalik towered over her, glowering.

"I didn't." But he wasn't entirely wrong. She'd never done anything to stop the collective.

"Liar! You were one of them. If it weren't for the fact you owed me wishes, you'd probably be with the other Shaitan right now, plotting world domination."

"For your information," she snapped, "I don't need to be anywhere close to you. I only need to supply the wishes once you make them. Other than that, I can go and be wherever I'd like."

"If that's true, then why are you here?"

"I don't know," she yelled. She really didn't.

"Children," Babette interjected, standing between them and holding out her hands. "Let's not fight."

"Did this dragonling just insult us?" Pride wasn't something the Jinn ever lacked. She turned a glare on the very young woman. At least she was young in comparison to the Jinn. "Weren't you taught to not interrupt your betters? As a matter of fact, given your lowly stature, you should be fetching us refreshments."

Babette gaped. "Excuse me? I am not a maid. A silver is—"

"Below a gold, who is well beneath a mage of any color," Maalik informed.

The dragoness, put in her place, sputtered, "Like fuck."

Jeebrelle put a hand on her arm. "Don't be so offended. It's only because you haven't been taught. In our time, mages were considered the rulers of our kind."

"Well, welcome to the twenty-first century where dragon mages have been essentially banished for being evil," Babette huffed angrily.

"And now we've returned. As it was foretold."

Babette snorted. "Good for you. Doesn't mean you get to suddenly leapfrog in position."

"You do realize I could crush you with a thought?" Maalik declared.

So could the Jinn.

But the dragoness didn't cower. Her chin tilted. "And that kind of attitude is why you mages got banished in the first place. Keep it up and I guarantee you'll be gone again. The king won't put up with that shit."

"Your king doesn't rule me." Maalik sneered.

"He does when you enter his territory. And keep in mind, an insult or threat to him is one to us all."

"And this is what I sacrificed for." Maalik stared at Babette then Jeebrelle. "I'm sorry. I should have left this generation to fend for itself."

"Yes, you should have," Jeebrelle agreed.

Maalik grimaced. "I made a mess of everything. I'm sorry. So very, very sorry. If I could turn back time, and change, I would." Maalik's shoulders slumped, and the Jinn wanted to hiss at the woman. Did she not see the way the man already shouldered too much blame?

"Guess it's not all bad. This era has some amenities that are quite unique."

"Then you should enjoy them," Maalik replied.

"I will, but not until I leave with what I came for."

"The ring was destroyed."

"I'm aware. Which is why we'll take the Jinn instead." Jeebrelle slewed a quick glance at his guest.

Maalik shook his head. "No. No one can have her until I'm done with her."

"Nunh-unh." Babette wagged a finger. "That's where you're wrong. See, I've got a teensy-tiny problem with you holding that nice little lady hostage. And taking away her clothes? Dude, that's some level of perv you've got going."

"She arrived in the nude. I told her to find garments," Maalik defended himself.

"Blame him not. I have no wish to wear any fabric. I am enjoying the sensation of air on my skin." It caused her nipples to tighten most delightfully.

"Nudism has a time and place. When out in public, you can't wander around in the buff. You'll get the cops called on you."

"Cops?" Her nose wrinkled at the odd word.

"Law enforcement. Because we have many laws that you have to obey," Babette informed.

"I am Jinn. Dragon laws don't apply."

"Actually, they're human rules."

That brought laughter. "Since when does anyone listen to anything they say?"

Babette's turn to look discomfited. "They've spread like a weed across the planet and outnumber us by the millions."

Millions… Astonished, the Jinn mouthed the word. It seemed impossible. Even at their most fractured, the Jinn never reached a thousand.

"Not only are they populous, they've harnessed technology," Jeebrelle confided. "They can do wondrous things with constructs that don't need magic to work."

"Such as?" the Jinn asked with curiosity.

"They've gone to the moon."

Her gaze rose to the stone ceiling. The moon was impossible to reach, even for a Jinn. If humans had indeed become that cunning, then she chilled at the thought of what could happen if the wrong one got hold of her. It had happened before. She'd been trapped by a man of power, who passed her down by setting her up to be captured by his son right after she granted the third wish. And then the son would release her and start the cycle once more. Generations they ruled using her. It took seducing a daughter to finally break that curse.

Maalik snorted. "Who was stupid enough to let them proliferate? Did none heed my warnings?"

"If you mean the whole kill-the-humans bit, the last time it happened, a betrayal led to them getting their hands on dracinore and almost wiping us out. We've only just barely recovered enough to deal with the fact humans know we exist," Babette informed.

"Because the dragons became weak after our

departure. Yet another thing I never saw," he grumbled.

"What do you see now, for this time and place?" Jeebrelle asked. "Is the world still in danger?"

"I don't know. The future is murky right now," Maalik admitted, shifting to show his true agitation.

Babette clapped her hands. "Well, once you figure it out, why not give Jeebs a holler? In the meantime, we'll just be leaving with the little lady."

"She is staying with me."

"I beg your pardon, but like fuck." Babette smiled. "See, here's the thing. You just punished her for three thousand years. Which is a pretty long sentence I'd say. Enough time to repent, maybe even have a total mental reset. Meaning, now that she's a free woman, she—not you—gets to decide where she goes. That's how justice works."

"She is Shaitan. She will cause harm," he insisted.

"So have your foretellings by the sound of it," Babette argued.

"I'm trying to save people. She's a killer." He pointed.

She defended her actions. "I'm obeying the magic that binds me to wishes." Most of the time at least. When she did lose her temper, fire was one of her ways to soothe the annoyance.

"So if no one makes a dumb wish, you won't hurt anyone, right?" Babette clarified.

"Only as long as no one attempts to harm me. I *will* defend myself."

"That sounds reasonable to me. To seal the deal, how about I treat you to something a little better than a dusty old cave? What do you say we go find a hotel? One with massive beds, lots of pillows, and soaker tubs. Maybe order in a massage and everything on the room service menu."

"That sounds nice." And she meant it. As a Jinn, she'd never experienced any of those things. Seen, yes, but a smoky being, always fearing capture, had no need for pleasures of the flesh.

"Sounds like we have a deal." Babette held out a hand, and the Jinn stared at it. "You're supposed to shake it," the dragoness added.

They clutched hands and pumped while Maalik protested, "You cannot bargain with a Shaitan."

"You're being rude. She has a name. Don't you?" Babette asked, eyeing her. "I'm Babette Silvergrace, by the way. Babs to my friends."

She blinked. It felt strange enough she did it again before saying, "I am Jinn."

"Which reminds me too much of the Borg. You need a name. Surely you have an identity of your own. A preference?"

She did, the name given to her by the female who'd eventually released her before her final capture by the dragon mages. A name she'd not used in thousands of years.

"My name is Daava."

"Nice to meet you." Babette shook her hand. "I take it you know Jeebs."

Daava arched a brow at the familiarity. "I know of her."

"Apparently more than I knew of you. I wasn't aware your kind could have a coherent thought, let alone speech." Jeebrelle frowned.

"It would seem then that a conversation is long overdue." Daava linked her arm with the plague mage. "Let me begin by asking, how did you get your hair to stay coiled on your head?"

Chapter Eight

The women were talking about braids.

Maalik didn't know if he should scream or laugh. Especially since they were quite serious in their conversation as they walked away from him, headed for a shimmering portal that had appeared. Jeebrelle's work and an indication they were about to leave.

"Hold on a moment." He interrupted their discussion of the over-under method. "Where do you think you're going?"

Babette skipped past him. "Somewhere that doesn't remind me of a horror movie where dead shit comes to life."

"You don't like it, then leave. She, however"—he indicated Daava's frame—"can't. I am owed two wishes."

Jeebrelle turned to eye him over her shoulder. "You want them so bad, then ask for them right now."

It almost killed him to say, "I can't." Because in the space of a few hours, he'd had his plan thrown for a loop.

"Until you know what you want, she's coming with me," Jeebrelle stated, stopping in front of the portal. "Ready?"

"Yes," Daava replied without once looking at him.

Unacceptable. There was only one thing to do given their adamancy.

"I'm coming, too." He moved to join them, only to have Babette hold up a hand.

"Just a second there, dude. You want to come for the ride, then you'll need to cough up payment."

He frowned. "You wish to be paid?"

"Not with money. We need something to cover her up." She pointed to Daava. "She'll draw attention if she shows up naked."

A very true statement. Maalik also found her distracting. "Where am I supposed to find a garment?" He swept a hand. "In case you hadn't noticed, there's not much around here to use, unless cobwebs would work?"

"Depends. Can you make them into a dress?"

"No."

"Why not? You're a wizard, aren't you? Can't you wave you hand and magic the dust into something?"

She made it sound simple. The conjuring of items out of nothing didn't just happen. If he wanted a dress, he had to basically steal one. But that required him knowing where to find one and then summoning it. In this time and place, he hadn't the slightest idea.

"I can't apparate clothing."

"Then you'll have to cough yours up."

"Cough? I don't understand."

Babette sighed. "I need your shirt."

He glanced at his chest. He didn't have his cloak. He'd shed it in the forge. He wore only one layer of thin linen. "If I give it, then I won't have a shirt."

"Which is fine. You won't get arrested for being bare chested. She will. So it's up to you. Help us out and join our merry band or refuse and stay in your cave by yourself."

"Why does it feel I have no choice?"

Babette grinned. "Because you don't. Now give it." Demanding fingers waggled.

He handed over his shirt and then wished he had another to cover himself, as the women, including the Jinn wearing his clothing, stared. It was Babette who muttered, "Damn. You've got enough muscle to tempt even me into going for a climb."

Daava licked her lips. "You kept fit during your confinement."

That had him puffing out his chest. He was, after all, still male, and his pride enjoyed the admiration in her gaze. "I wanted to be ready for when we emerged."

Jeebrelle cleared her throat. "Can you ogle him later? My portal is losing stability." The warning had them moving quickly in and through the cold path that led them to an alley that stunk of urine and garbage.

"Oh, what's that smell?" Daava gagged and, to his surprise, tucked into him, pressing her nose against his chest.

He almost wrapped an arm around her protectively. Instead, he gruffly replied, "This world isn't the cleanest."

"Are the citizens too lazy to burn their garbage?" Daava tilted her head to glance at him, her nose wrinkled in disgust.

"They believe this slow, odorous decay is better than a clean burn."

"They are mistaken." Daava pointed, and the

large metal container beside them suddenly smoked as the garbage within ignited.

"There is much in this world that you will find perturbing," he declared. He was still adjusting to the differences from his time.

Honk. Honk.

"What is that?" Daava asked.

"Just traffic," Babette announced, heading to the mouth of the alley and peeking out.

"It's loud." Daava put her hands over her ears as a vehicle blared once more.

"As mentioned, the world has become populous and has advanced technologically since our departure," Maalik advised. He still remembered the culture shock when he emerged to a world he didn't recognize anymore.

"It's very unpleasant thus far." Daava remained unimpressed.

"You get used to it," Jeebrelle declared. "And parts of it are good. Wait until you try a wondrous thing called a Big Mac."

"Pizza and Twinkies are the two best things to eat in the world," Babette interjected. "And I will introduce you to them both once we get somewhere safe."

"There is danger?" Maalik asked. He'd been

wandering since their release and had not come across any threats worth noting.

"Pretty sure you don't want to go viral because you're like a walking ad for Thunder Down Under and she's Playboy material. You're going to draw attention. The wrong kind, which I usually enjoy, but now is not the time."

Indeed, many eyes appeared fixed upon them as they emerged onto a sidewalk made of that poured stone they called concrete. The doors to the hotel were comprised mostly of glass and framed in a gold-hued metal with a high shine. Inside were marble floors, high ceilings, and chandeliers hung with hundreds of glass pendants. No candles or lanterns. The world ran on electricity now, which he understood to be like the charge found in a thunderstorm.

Babette handled affairs with the staff and in short order had them ensconced in their temporary quarters. The room they offered him held luxury like he would have never imagined with a carpet underfoot, a large bed, a divan, a plush chair, and even its own oubliette with the promised hot water.

Since his arrival in this time, Maalik had been living for the most part in remote spots by water sources, stealing what he needed to survive. In retrospect, he couldn't have said why he'd been depriving himself. Mages used to live better than kings. Rulers bowed to them. They had whatever they wanted.

But that was then. This was now.

He'd survived the imprisonment spell. Now he just needed to atone, the how being the problem. He'd really thought it would be as simple as going back in time. He'd pinpointed the spots where he'd made the biggest mistakes. Fix those and everything could turn out right.

But he couldn't travel into the past, leaving him with what choice? He owed it to his brethren to do something. Especially Ellona. She'd died unhappy because of him.

If she'd actually died…

He'd never found her body, just the note by the bottomless crevice. What if the reason his first wish failed was because Ellona lived? It would be the simplest explanation.

Was there a way to find out that didn't involve wasting a wish? Thinking of which, there was some anxiety at being separated from the Jinn and not only because she owed him two boons. He found himself concerned about her wellbeing. Contrary to his recollection of the Shaitan, Daava appeared vulnerable, capable of reasoning and thought. It made him wonder if that had always been the case.

His visions had shown him many things when it came to the Jinn and later the Shaitan. Violence, first and foremost. Fire, so much burning and death. But did that come before or after the dragon mages began chasing them down? Daava hinted the latter, and he couldn't exactly say she was wrong.

His choices made a difference. If only he'd not been so selfish.

Exiting from the bathroom in a cloud of steam, he almost uttered an unmanly cry as he came face to face with Daava.

"What are you doing in my room?" he yelped. Never mind he'd just been thinking of her. Having her this close to him had a hardening effect on his body, especially since she moved closer.

"Save me," she whispered.

"From who?" A protective instinct immediately roused.

She tucked against his chest, her lips moving on his skin as she said, "Save me from those savages. They want to cut my hair."

The horror! "Tell them no."

"The young one said something about split ends, and then, as she threatened with a giant pair of scissors, expected me to wear some contraption to conceal my breasts."

"For a society that allows its females to wear

sparse amounts of clothing and pants, they have odd ideas about the body. Do you know the men are expected to wear binding clothing around their groins?" he confided.

"Really?" The remark had her gaze lowering to the towel wrapped around his waist, a damp piece of fabric that threatened to fall as a part of him nudged in interest. He shifted away from Daava.

"If you don't wish for them to dress and groom you, then tell them so."

"I did." Her lips turned down. "They are very insistent."

"And you let them live?" Said lightly and yet with curiosity. As Shaitan went, she didn't act as expected.

"I'm not a murderous monster."

"Then I guess you're getting a haircut."

She scowled. "You're not helping."

"You're the one who decided you wanted to leave with them," he pointed out.

"I didn't know they'd do this."

"Guess you regret not staying in my cave." A smug note to the statement.

Her nose wrinkled. It was adorable. Distracting. Since meeting her, he'd barely thought of Ellona.

"That cave was beyond uncomfortable, and you know it."

"I do."

"Hence why you begged to leave."

"I didn't beg," he retorted with a touch of indignation. Okay, a lot of it.

"You gave up your shirt."

"Ever think the bed and hot water proved impossible to resist?"

Her lips curved. "I wouldn't know. I've yet to try either. I escaped while they were still discussing what torture to inflict on me."

"Then use mine." He thought nothing of offering, only to realize too late she might accept.

"I don't want to sleep yet."

"Then bathe. There is another towel for drying when you are done." He gestured, and Daava entered the bathing chamber, only to emerge a moment later.

"How do I get the water to come out?"

He knew better than to laugh. He'd had the same dilemma. "It's actually quite ingenious," he said, moving to help her.

She was just as amazed as him when she saw the turn of a knob brought hot water. He shifted to grab some of the soap from the sink, and when he turned around, it was to gape, as she stood sleek and tempting under the spray, face lifted to the water. Eyes closed. Mouth open. Her hair slick down her back, meaning he had the full effect of her naked body.

Gulp.

He closed his eyes, but it was too late. The image was burned into his mind. He fled, only to find himself face to face with Jeebrelle, who arched a brow.

"Getting cozy with the Jinn?"

"It's not what you think. She needed help with the shower."

"Come with me," Jeebrelle ordered. "I think it's time we had a talk."

He knew that tone. The one that said he was in big trouble. And what did the mighty mage do?

He hung his head and followed.

Chapter Nine

Daava basked in the hot water. She'd never had a shower before. Didn't need to when she existed as smoke. Dirt didn't cling to her. She'd never understood what it was to be grimy until she was made flesh.

And how did that happen? No doubt it had something to do with Maalik's wish. She just didn't understand where it went wrong. What would it take to return to her normal self?

Did she even want to?

There was something intense about having an actual body. The sensations were unlike anything she could have imagined. Even better, the fire in the alley proved that she still had magic to use. Perhaps she'd remain flesh for a while. Partake of the delights to be had.

Eventually, her skin took on a strange texture and she shut off the water. The towel provided a friction on her flesh and then formed a sarong that rapidly got heavy in the back as her wet hair soaked into it. Perhaps trimming it would be more convenient. At least until she got back her smoky body.

If she got it back.

There was something to be said for having a solid nature. The sensations bombarding her at every turn were a sensory delight. Sight, smell, touch. She'd never experienced so much.

And she wanted more.

Upon exiting the bathing chamber, her good mood faltered as she took in the tableau.

Maalik appeared grim and annoyed as he sat on the divan across from Jeebrelle, who'd taken over the chair. He flicked Daava a glance that returned and smoldered for a moment before his gaze shuttered into something flat and unreadable.

"About time. I was thinking you might have drowned," he drawled.

"Can I drown?" It was never an issue before.

He looked like he would speak but instead huffed a breath.

"Join us," Jeebrelle demanded. "I have some questions for you."

"They'll have to wait," Babette announced,

suddenly appearing with an armful of fabric. "I've got clothes for Daava and that," she said, turning her head a moment before a knock at the door, "is our food."

Having never eaten, Daava had her doubts as to whether she should. Ingesting was a thing animals did. However, the moment the smells hit her nose all her qualms disappeared. Her mouth watered, and her stomach made the oddest gurgling sound.

She ate. And ate. Each mouthful was a pleasure that had her groaning and chewing and looking for more until she couldn't fit in any more food, her belly rounded with satiety. She leaned back to see three sets of eyes staring.

"Did I grow a third eye?" She patted herself to check. Having once done it for a master who said he needed an eye in the back of his head to watch for enemies, the possibility existed.

"Just wondering how you might feel about entering a food competition. First place in the pie-eating contest is pie for a year. I love pie." Babette, for some reason, said the last in Jeebrelle's direction.

"You must compete to eat? Survival of the fittest. A worthy game to play," Daava said with a nod.

"You know, your English is awfully good for someone hidden away inside a ring for three thousand years. As is yours," Babette accused, swinging her gaze to Maalik.

"I spent the first few days teaching myself about this world," he explained.

"But she just got out. When did she learn?"

Daava eyed the remains of food on the tray. "While I rested within my prison, I heard voices. Sometimes even music and song."

"Who guarded the ring before I acquired it?" Maalik queried.

"The Silvergrace family owned it until you stole it from us," Babette accused.

"But obviously didn't have it secured. The outside world, or at least the noise from it, penetrated the ring," Jeebrelle mused aloud.

It made sense to Daava. And also roused her curiosity. "There was a prince I used to hear. A prince from Bel Air."

Babette snickered. "That would be Will Smith. Epic babe and probably the fault of Ada. She used to have the hugest crush on him. Until she got married. Now she's only got eyes for her husband." Babette rolled her orbs, making Daava smile. "Want to see a picture?"

The Will Smith was very handsome, also very married. Babette showed her many images of actors, those playing parts in plays that could be seen around the world by all people, not just those who could afford to attend a show.

Daava's stomach gurgled, and she burped.

Jeebrelle appeared startled. Maalik dropped his jaw, but Babette laughed and said, "Compliments to the chef."

As Daava debated having one more bite now that she had room, Maalik muttered, "I still don't know how someone so tiny can eat so much."

Self-conscious—yet another new feeling—she ducked her head. "Is eating always so pleasurable?"

"If the cooking is good, then yes. But surely you've…" Maalik trailed off. "How do Jinn feed?"

Her shoulders rolled. "We don't exactly. We get what we need from the world around us. There is an energy in the air that rejuvenates."

"Sounds dull and tasteless. Give me vanilla frosting," Babette said, whipping out yet another of her special cakes.

Daava had to admit she understood the love of them. Sugar was a delight on her tongue.

Less pleasant? The pressure in her lower body. She squirmed enough Babette frowned in her direction. "Do you have to pee?"

"Of course not," she haughtily claimed, only to wonder.

"Have you ever peed?" Babette rephrased.

"No. Jinn don't have bodily functions."

"What about those with bodies, though?" Maalik queried.

She pondered it for a moment. Did wearing the flesh include all the functions?

"Go sit on the toilet," Babette suggested. "See what happens."

What happened was she made water and then something came out of her that was just foul. So foul she had another shower, her towel from before warm and dry with a snap of her fingers.

When she emerged wrapped in it, only Maalik remained.

"Feeling okay?" he asked.

"No." Gone was her good humor of before. Irritable, and not just because of her sore stomach and bottom, she grumbled, "My eyes are uncomfortable, and my mouth keeps opening wide and exhaling."

"It's called a yawn because you're tired."

The very idea! "Jinn don't sleep."

"Give it a try. Worse thing that can happen is it won't work."

"You mean lie in a bed?"

"That's usually where people sleep. And before you say you're not people, right now, you're wearing the body of one."

She glanced down. "I am tired." Stated almost as a question followed by her lying down on the nearest bed.

He protested. "That's mine."

"There's room enough for you on the other side," she muttered, closing her eyes.

"I don't know why I should have to share," he complained, even as he slid onto the mattress beside her.

He pulled at the blankets, and it took her a moment before she understood his intent. She snuggled deep into the pillow with the sheets drawn over her, making her warm, if uncomfortable in the damp towel. She removed it and sent a bit of magic to dry and warm the fabric around her.

"Ah." She sighed. "This is nice. How do I sleep?"

"Just keep your eyes closed and try to think of nothing," he advised.

The first part? Easy. The latter? Her mind whirled. So much had happened. But her body was tired. Soon, she slept, and slipped into her first dream.

Chapter Ten

Maalik woke to Daava whimpering.

"What's wrong?" he asked, only to realize she was asleep. She must be dreaming, for she thrashed and cried out again.

He should ignore it. What did he care if she suffered from nightmares? She was Shaitan, a soulless, unfeeling monster. As if anything could hurt her. He'd fought the Jinn. Cut their smoky bodies into ribbons and watched them heal before he managed his next swing. It wasn't easy to break them into pieces, especially as the Shaitan grew in stature, going from the easy-to-trap Ifrit and Jinn to a large foe who didn't allow itself to be stuffed into a bottle without a fight.

Should he have put her into a bottle and only

brought her out when he needed her? He winced. That sounded cold even by his standards.

A low moan drew his attention once more to Daava. She murmured and twitched in her sleep. A sharp cry escaped her, high pitched with pain. Maalik couldn't help himself. He reached for her, his hand on her bare arm, the only touch needed to suddenly fling him elsewhere.

In the space of a breath, he found himself suddenly not in his bed anymore but standing in a sandstone building. The blocks comprising the walls were almost seamlessly joined to create a large room, a wealthy one judging by the fine things he could see. Rugs covered the floor. Tapestries and murals brightened the walls. The décor seemed familiar and yet alien at the same time. It had been three thousand years, after all, since he'd seen the accoutrements of his time.

Where am I? For he didn't recall having ever been in this place.

But Daava had.

He spotted her, kneeling by a hearth, not the flesh and skin version he'd come to know, but the smoke that used to comprise her presence. It retained the same female shape, if in a posture of defeat he'd yet to see in her. With him, she boldly met his gaze, teased, even challenged.

Not this version with its head bowed, hands tucked in her lap. Her hair hung in lifeless wisps of fog, tattered and sickly. A chain hung from the thick collar placed around her insubstantial neck. He didn't need to touch it to feel the forged dracinore and the power coursing through it. Inscribed upon it were magical glyphs that he imagined comprised a spell that kept her imprisoned. A version of what they'd done with the seals.

A man with a corpulent frame and florid complexion stood over Daava, mouth flapping, hands gesturing, as he harangued. The dialect was unfamiliar and yet the angry intent clear.

Daava cowered before the yelling man and, when her submissive pose didn't appease, threw herself prostrate. The man's ire didn't lessen. The angry man kicked, and to Maalik's surprise, the blow connected with Daava's chest. She grunted.

Maalik gaped. The magical collar didn't just tether her. It gave her an actual presence, which meant she could be harmed.

The male withdrew a poker he had resting in the coals. Surely he wouldn't...

Having been raised in this era, Maalik knew the man would. He still muttered, "No."

The man didn't hear him, but it was as if Daava did. She glanced at him, and in that moment, he didn't see the enemy or a Jinn. He saw a woman tortured and in pain. Someone who'd given up.

"It's a dream. Don't let it happen." He tried to move toward her, but each step drew him no closer, as if he walked in place.

Unable to act, he could only watch in horror as the man took the poker and pressed it to her smoke-solid body.

She screamed.

Maalik yelled, pounded against the shield of the memory, unable to make it stop. He could only watch and listen as Daava screamed herself hoarse and then sobbed.

The process repeated over and over through the years. The scenes whipped by in a blur that showed her progression, starting out defiant then becoming so beaten she no longer even raised her head when her current master arrived. A male who'd gotten rich and fat off his wishes. As he dragged a young boy along with him, he limped from the gout swelling his limbs. His teeth were rotted from sweets. Unhealthy to the extreme with one wish left.

"Make me young and healthy again."

The moment the male made his request, accompanied by the slash of a knife over an unsuspecting throat, Maalik could see the magic as it drained from Daava faster than she could handle.

Her dark smoke shape lightened and thinned to the point he thought for sure she'd evaporate.

Could a wish kill a Jinn if it asked too much? He honestly didn't know, especially since she couldn't defend herself while she wore that collar. She fell to the floor and spasmed in the growing puddle of blood. He could see her very essence draining until she lay prone.

Dead?

A twitch showed she lived. The boy brought along as a sacrifice didn't.

When the wish considered itself completed, it left behind a man young in appearance. Fit.

Barely a shadow on the floor, Daava managed to mumble, "You have your three wishes. Release me."

"You'll be released once I find the right buyer." The man cackled and took his new young self out of the house to enjoy his new body.

Maalik shouted, "Let her go. You've had enough. She's fulfilled her bargain."

"As if appealing to his sense of morality will work now." The sarcasm had him whirling to see a wan Daava staring at him.

"What is this? What's happening?"

"As if you don't know. This is my past."

"Why am I seeing it?"

"Why am I seeing you?" she countered. Only before he could reply, her attention turned to the door. "Here comes the next part."

The man had returned, young and grinning. So pleased with himself as he and the stranger he'd brought walked around Daava, hands moving as rapidly as their speech as they negotiated her sale.

A deal was struck, and as the newly young man went to spit on it, the other pulled a knife. Greed and cruelty repaid with death. The lifeless eyes stared in wide surprise as the blood spread. Daava scuttled out of its reach, the chain jangling with the movement.

The killer reached for the metal links and yanked.

Dragged into the light, she begged, "Please, set me free."

"I intend to, Jinn." The new owner rescued her from the collar, and the cycle of wishes started over —along with the abuse.

By the time Maalik snapped out of Daava's nightmare, he understood why the Shaitan wanted revenge on the world. To be sorely used, over and over… And now, he did the same. Perhaps without the collar and the beatings, but at the same time, he took away her choice. Would drain her for his own purpose.

It left him with a sour taste. The body in his arms shifted, making him aware they were in bed. Both awake. Aware.

Daava held her breath, as if she were alive. Was she? She certainly felt real and solid in his arms. Also, very naked, something he tried to ignore.

"I know you're awake," he murmured softly. "Are you okay?"

"Why wouldn't I be?"

"You were having a nightmare."

The statement had her turning in his grip until she faced him. "I don't dream."

"You do." He hesitated before adding, "I was in the nightmare with you. I saw what your previous masters did."

She said nothing, just stared at him.

It discomfited. "It was cruel and wrong."

"Yet no one stopped them. Jinn had no rights. No say."

"I don't understand how it happened, though. They were humans."

"Clever humans who like to experiment. It is because of them I became what you call a Shaitan. They discovered the size of a Jinn affected the power of a wish. They began to assemble us, even as they kept us trapped."

"With the collar. How did they create it?"

Her lips thinned. "It is my belief they had help."

"From who?"

"No one originating here."

"Is the collar still around?" he asked.

Anger sparked in her gaze. "Why?" She turned it into something sensual. "Are you into the kinky types of fornication, mage? Many of my masters found it titillating to string me up to have their way."

Rage filled him at the reminder. "I ask because it should be destroyed. No one should ever suffer like you did." He meant it. He might have fought the Shaitan, and yet, he didn't believe in torture.

"Would you really destroy the collar?" she said with lilting surprise.

"Yes."

She laughed. "I find that hard to believe coming from the man who devised the prisons that cursed us for so long."

"Would you have preferred death?"

"I would prefer to just be allowed to exist without being used for my magic."

"And what would you do if you weren't granting wishes?" It should have been sarcastic, not rhetorical.

"Experience life. While I was relaxing in the

ring, I spent time reflecting on the things I'd never done."

"Such as?"

"I never rode a camel."

"Nasty creatures. Better you stick to the carpets you're fond of. Surely you have more interesting things you want to try."

"I'd like to read every book ever published."

"A lofty goal that will leave little time for world domination."

"I never wanted to rule the world. But the attacks on the Jinn wouldn't stop. We had to do something."

"So you were going to unleash a destroyer of all life to fix that?"

"You have to understand that we don't have the same concept of life as you do. For us, its magic that feeds. It's all we need. Or so I thought. Having a body is providing me with a different perspective."

"Because you can feel," he surmised.

"Until recently, I never ate, slept, or wore clothes. My physical interactions occurred while wearing the collar and were primarily pain and discomfort."

"That's…" He paused because there was no justification. "Horrible."

"It was," she replied softly, her gaze dropping from his to a spot below his chin.

The silence that fell only served to heighten his awareness of her and the realization they were both in bed together. Both were nude because she'd lost her towel and he never wore clothes to sleep.

Her body pressed against his. His cock, trapped between their bodies, went from soft to hard and throbbed against her lower belly. It didn't care he was in bed with the enemy. It sensed an attractive woman.

"I am feeling odd," she stated suddenly.

"Odd how?" Because he had no problem identifying the fact he was aroused. Almost painfully so. Cheater. He held himself still and thought of Ellona. Only her face wouldn't come to mind.

Daava's did.

Chapter Eleven

The shock of wanting Daava almost had him pulling away.

Almost.

Maybe if there'd been any blood left in his body, he'd have been able to think rationally, but he throbbed. A pent-up desire that thousands of years of masturbation wouldn't deny.

Daava squirmed and tensed as she said, "There is a strange sensation between my legs. And I am wet. As if I am leaking."

"Uh." He had nothing to say because his tongue was stuck. How to explain what she felt?

"It doesn't feel like I need to make waste," she mused. She also rubbed a little more against him, obviously trying to kill him.

"The wetness you feel, it's, um, because…er, of

—ah—desire." He, the mighty seer and ancient dragon mage, stammering.

"Desire? As in for sex?" She sounded surprised. "I have had sex before. It never felt like this."

"Because that was rape." It emerged on a growl.

"You make that sound bad."

"It is bad because you had no choice. It was done to impose power and shame and pain."

"It was the plight of all who were slaves in that time."

"Doesn't make it right." Her acceptance only made it worse. "It's also sad."

"How is it sad?"

"Because, for all your experience, you've obviously never felt desire."

"Does it make a difference?"

He shifted against her and trailed light fingers down her bare back, making her shiver before saying, "You tell me. Do you feel good or bad right now?"

She concentrated for the moment. "Good, but that is probably because you are not attempting to impale me."

It took a moment to understand what kind of impaling she meant. "The, um, penetration of a phallus can be enjoyable if those participating are ready and willing." This had to be the most awkward and strangest conversation of his life.

"Perhaps. The humans certainly indulge in it often enough. I've even seen some females who take enjoyment in being stabbed by the male appendage."

It shouldn't have been funny, and yet he couldn't help a hint of wry amusement. "It's hardly stabbing. The woman survives."

"Obviously, given that is how children are created." She shifted against him. "You wish to stab me."

"Uh." Yes, yes, he did. What was wrong with him? He shouldn't be thinking about fornicating with anyone, let alone a Shaitan. "This is wrong."

He began to pull away, only to have her wrap herself tight around him.

"Why do you appear angry?"

"I'm not angry," he snapped.

"You are. Because you desire me." She showed an unexpected astuteness.

Hard to deny with his erection pressing against her belly. "I shouldn't."

"Then don't."

"It's not that easy."

"If you wish to stab me, then do it. Perhaps I will understand why some find it enjoyable given, unlike previous experiences, I'm finding it strangely exhilarating thus far." She squirmed against him, and he groaned.

"Are you in pain?"

"Yes," he hissed. He ached, balls, cock, and heart.

"Can I assist you?"

It would be so easy. She'd admitted to being wet already. He could just slide in and…

And take advantage since Daava had no real concept of choice. In her mind, he was her master. If she didn't do as he wished, she probably worried he'd hurt her. As if he'd ever force anyone.

He began to withdraw, but once more, she held on.

"You are angry again."

"I'm—" Actually, he was, and he couldn't explain why other than it bothered him to know she'd never known a kind and gentle touch. Never experienced true pleasure, just selfishness.

"I'm going to touch you," he announced.

"You already are," she reminded.

"Intimately. If you don't like it, tell me to stop." He slid his hand down, trailing it over her spine to her waist then her hips.

"It tickles," she said with a giggle.

"Good. Lie on your back."

"Will you tickle me more? I like it when you touch me."

Forget moving away. "I'm going to use more than just my hands now."

"Ooh." She rolled and lay still. He hesitated only a second before sliding under the blanket and positioning himself over her. His breath fanned hotly across her skin, and he heard her say a tad breathlessly, "This is pleasant."

"Only pleasant?"

"I feel stiff and trembly all at once."

"Because you're aroused." And so was he. He'd been without for so long.

He blew hotly on the nipple hiding under the blanket.

She shivered.

He ran his lips over the nub.

"Oh." She trembled.

He tugged the tip of her breast with his mouth, and she arched her body. A sign she enjoyed herself, confirmed when he slid his hand down through the softness of the curls on her mound to the haven between her thighs. He found her wet.

His finger spread the petals of her sex and stroked, drawing gasps and shortening her breath into pants. A finger went in, and she clenched him. He kept sucking at her nipple as he fingered her. He slid a second digit inside her channel while his thumb rubbed her nub.

He'd barely started playing when her body went rigid. The fingers he had within felt her quiver and tighten as she came, ripples of orgasm that had him throbbing fiercely.

"Oh. My." She exhaled. "What was that?"

"You climaxed." There was pride in giving her the first one.

"As in we had sex?" Her tone got high pitched.

"Of a sort."

"But you didn't stab me."

Not because he didn't want to. "Fornication takes many forms, but it should always feel good."

"Did it feel good for you?"

Yes, even though he ached. He wanted nothing more than to give her another example. To show her how stabbing could also make her orgasm.

It had been so long since he'd been intimate with anyone. Did he really want to break the drought with his enemy? He had to get away from her before he did the unthinkable.

Maalik rolled out of bed hard enough he hit the floor with a thud and groaned.

"Are you injured?" A glance showed a pair of dark eyes peering back from a tangled mane of hair. She looked nothing like a killer Shaitan.

Smelled better than any flower. How would she taste?

What is wrong with me? Perhaps there was some kind of seduction spell being emitted by her arousal. Or maybe he should just admit he was a man with needs.

He couldn't help it; he laughed.

"What's so funny?"

A few things, starting with him obviously having lost his mind since he wanted nothing more than to crawl back into bed with her and finish what he started. "Your hair. You are going to hate brushing it out."

She sat upright, her messy mane only partially hiding her nude body. "What about my hair?" She dragged her fingers into the knots and screeched. "Ouch. What's wrong? Why does it hurt?"

"You've got knots. You need a good brushing."

"I'm thinking perhaps scissors." She glared at a particularly gnarly section.

"Hold off on the massacre. Let's get some clothes on, and then we can find you a comb."

"A comb has smaller prongs than my fingers." She held them out. "How is that supposed to hurt less?"

"Never said it wouldn't hurt a little. Maybe a lot. But you'll survive."

"Your words aren't encouraging. I'd rather have no pain." She scampered from the bed and ran to stand in front of the mirror, giving him an interesting view of her posterior.

Before he could imagine it bent over, he scrambled to find clothes, delivered the night before while Daava stuffed her mouth with everything she could find.

The pants and shirt went on, but he kept his feet bare as he headed for Daava. who stood in front of the mirror. He handed her a shirt. "Put this on."

"Must I?"

"Yes." If only for his own peace of mind.

The shirt did little to hide her sexy nature. As he moved past her to the bathing chamber, he caught something strange in the reflection she stared at.

He turned to more properly glance and then gaped at what he saw. "You're giving yourself different hairstyles." The reflection showed Daava sporting a multitude of coiffures.

"I like this one best." The mirror showed Daava wearing her hair just past her shoulders, smooth and unadorned but for the tiny braid that started at her temple and circled round.

"Very nice but I'm not a hairdresser."

"I can create it with magic." Her brow creased, and her tongue poked out as her hair suddenly frizzed and emitted a static charge that had him retreating.

Strands began to fall, then hunks. The air filled with a sizzling noise that was accompanied by the stench of burning hair. It didn't last long, and when finished, Daava stood perfectly coiffed.

She smiled in the mirror. "That's better."

"You used magic rather than a comb? Isn't that wasteful?"

"It didn't take much."

"What about the mirror show before that?"

She made a noise. "Reflections are an easy cast."

The statement gave him an idea. "Easy enough it wouldn't count as a wish?"

Daava cocked her head. "You want to see something."

"Someone."

"Ellona." Daava said the name softly, and he couldn't have said why his cheeks heated.

"Yes, Ellona. Can you show me? I just want to know she's alive and okay."

Daava's fingers trailed over the glass. "I could. Although it will be difficult since I've never met her. I don't suppose you have a token that belonged to her?"

He shook his head. "Just my memories."

"And a lingering love. It might be enough. Give me your hand." Daava reached for it and pushed his palm flat onto the mirror. She kept hers atop and murmured softly, "Concentrate on the one you love."

The one he loved. For a second, his mind flashed to nothing then to Daava. Shocked, he opened his eyes, and there she was staring back via her reflection.

Chapter Twelve

"You don't appear to be thinking of your lover," Daava remarked.

"How does me thinking of Ellona help? Are you reading my mind?" Maalik stiffened, ready to pull away.

"More like boosting it. You think of the one you love, which creates a connection, allowing us to see her in the mirror."

"Sounds easy." In the reflection he towered over Daava, but she didn't cower. Rather she appeared comfortable with him. Moments ago, in bed, she'd even trusted him.

"It is easy. Just think of her."

He closed his eyes and tried to picture Ellona, only to realize he couldn't clearly remember her face. He thought of the good times, which were few and far between once they'd been in the tunnels for a while. The more he tried to recollect, the more the good was overshadowed by the bad.

So much bad.

He'd done his best to forget the fighting and recriminations. The fact became clear that they did better as a couple when they could spend long times apart. Within the cave system, there was nowhere to escape. No one else to turn to for a while, and even when they did manage to find each other, petty quarrels sent them fleeing. It shouldn't have surprised him Ellona chose to leave. After all, by that time, they hadn't been intimate in a long time. Barely spoke unless it was for her to hiss how much she hated him.

Daava must have sensed his agitation. "Calm yourself and float on thoughts of the one you love. The one you wished back into existence."

Was it time to admit that for all he'd done for Ellona, it wasn't out of love? It was more like guilt and nostalgia for something they never truly had.

A peek at the mirror showed nothing unless he counted the frown on Daava's face.

"It's not working," he stated.

She bit her lip. "Which is odd, because my magic is responding."

"Probably my fault. My mind isn't cooperating.

Maybe we can try again later."

"Maybe. Or…"

She didn't finish, so he prodded. "Or, what?"

"Perhaps she truly is dead and that's why we can't see her." Daava sounded hesitant even suggesting it.

"If that's true, then what about my wish?"

"Could be that your first wish did something different than requested."

"Different how? I had a pretty specific request."

She frowned. "Actually, what you asked for was for the woman you love to be brought into existence."

He didn't hear it at first, but once he replayed the words in his head, it struck. "I never specified that woman to be Ellona." And given magic could be very precise, that might have had an effect. "If that wish didn't bring Ellona back, then who? Who else do I love?"

For some reason, they stared at each other in the mirror. He remembered that moment in bed when she'd responded to his touch. He stepped closer so that his body brushed hers. Her lips parted.

Before anything further could happen, the door to the other room slammed open and Babette bounded through, wide-eyed with excitement.

"Dudes! You gotta see this. Some crazy dragoness has taken over the CN Tower in downtown Toronto."

They followed Babette to her room where Jeebrelle sat cross-legged on a bed, balancing a machine called a laptop that could scry events. Videos, those of this age called it. A technology that didn't require magic but was most incredible. The screen showed an aerial view of a city.

"Have you possessed a bird?" Daava asked as she neared.

"Not quite. That live feed you're watching is coming from a drone," Babette declared, flopping onto the bed, sending the laptop wobbling.

Once it steadied, they saw the drone appeared to be aiming for a tall spire of a building. As it rose in altitude, the scrying image showed a massive shape curled in repose. The polished scales caught the sparkle of the afternoon sun.

Only one dragon Maalik ever met possessed metal scales.

Ellona.

A lithe form, sleek and distinctive, with a pair of delicate horns sharp as spears, leaped from the building and flew directly at the drone sending them pictures. The dragon opened its mouth wide and swallowed it whole.

Chapter Thirteen

"Ellona's alive," Maalik stated, and yet he didn't appear overjoyed.

He wasn't alone. After a day, night, and morning of incredible wonder, Daava felt her happiness shrinking.

"You know that dragon?" Babette asked, turning to glance at Maalik.

"We both do," Jeebrelle softly interjected. "That's Ellona. One of the thirteen."

"A sixth dragon mage?" Babette blinked. "Okay, this is starting to get a bit crazy. I thought there were only supposed to be four horse dudes of the apocalypse?"

Jeebrelle addressed Maalik. "It appears your wish came true. You brought her back to life." Her last statement held an incredulous note.

But Daava quickly countered, "Impossible. Necromancy is the most difficult thing to do and requires much sacrifice, not to mention a fresh body. If she's alive, it's because she was never dead."

"It appears our assessment of those who survived might have been flawed. I take it you didn't know?" Jeebrelle still only addressed Maalik.

He roused himself from his shock enough to say, "No, I had no idea. I saw the note Ellona left by the bottomless crevice and assumed she'd taken her life."

"We all did." Jeebrelle paused the image on the odd contraption and did something to reverse time so that they could all clearly see the dragon. Big, but nothing close to as large as Maalik.

"Are you sure that's your Ellona?" Daava peered more closely, trying to find a link or familiarity. Had her magic somehow brought Ellona back?

Maalik had no doubt about the dragon. He pointed to the screen. "Where is that place? How do I get there?"

Babette had the answer. "Depends on how fast you want to get there. Can't exactly take a plane, unless you've got a passport. Flying while in dragon form? You're looking at eight, ten hours, not counting rest stops. If by car, train, or bus, a few days probably and you'd still have problems at the border without an ID."

"I'll need directions. Can you show me where this Toronto is on a map?" Portals required first-hand knowledge of the location and care in creating them lest a person materialize inside a wall. A horrible way to die.

He leaned down, and Jeebrelle showed him a map so he could plan a route. Daava left, returning to the other room to pace, agitated, and yet she couldn't say why.

Having followed, Babette caught her scowling. "Why the frown, dudette?"

"I'm not frowning."

"Then you're smiling upside down."

She huffed. "I don't mean to frown. I'm not sure why I'm feeling anything at all."

"Don't tell me you're going to miss the big jerk?"

The very idea surprised. "Is that why I am irritable of a sudden?"

"Let's see, how do you feel about him leaving?"

Daava grimaced. "I shouldn't care. Yet I do. Why?"

"You like him."

"I do, and yet I shouldn't. He is my sworn

enemy. He wants nothing more than to use me for the wishes I can grant."

"Are you sure that's all he feels? I got the impression he was into you."

Daava blinked.

"Into you as in the way a guy likes a woman," Babette explained.

"Many men and woman alike have desired me."

"What about you? Have you desired them?"

Her lips pursed. "He is the only one I've ever had an interest in pursuing. And after his lesson in pleasure earlier, I wouldn't be averse to him bringing me to climax again."

Babette's eyes widened far enough Daava feared she might lose them. "He made you come?"

"If by come you mean orgasm for the first time, then yes. I now understand the interest in fornication."

This time, Babette's mouth rounded. "Are all Jinn this honest?"

"There is no purpose in lying to you. I owe you nothing. You want nothing of me that I am aware of. You are willing to impart your knowledge, and I find myself in need of advice given these types of emotional issues are new to me and thus require study."

"You are nothing like the other genies I've run

into. Which is a good thing I might add," Babette exclaimed.

"And you're not as arrogant as I recall the dragons being."

"I'm kind of insulted. I am plenty arrogant." Babette lifted her chin and put her hands on her hips.

"Trust me when I say you are personable in comparison to many I've known."

"Yeah, well, lesbian here, and I learned as a teen that it sucks to be judged by some general opinion rather than on merit."

"If only your ancestors had followed that same lesson."

"Speaking of ancestors, I am still having a hard time wrapping my head around the fact that you are into Maalik. I mean he's the reason you were locked up. Shouldn't you hate his guts and want to rip them from his body and eat them?"

"Firstly, that doesn't sound appetizing. Secondly, it seems like a waste of time. I didn't wait that long to emerge from my prison to immediately immerse myself into strife." Besides, while she didn't condone his reasons, she understood them. The Jinn would have killed his world with the Iblis.

"So what is your plan?" Babette asked.

"I don't have one. For the moment, I can only wait for Maalik to request his last two wishes."

"What about when that's done? You'll be free?"

Daava wrinkled her nose. "Will I?" Every time she hoped, and every single time she ended up caught back in that vicious wishing cycle.

"You only have to give wishes if you're released from some kind of prison, meaning don't get captured," Babette declared.

"You say that as if it's easy, and yet, the longest I've ever been free was while I was inside that ring."

"Was it horrible?"

"Honestly, it was probably the most peaceful I've ever been." Unlike the dragon mages who'd been aware the entire time, she spent it in a cloudy limbo of reflection, calm, and the occasional voices that came as if from beyond a great distance.

"You almost sound as if you miss it."

In a way, she did. "Inside the ring, there were no expectations of me. I wasn't part of a collective with my choice removed. I wasn't hunted. Or drained until I couldn't hold myself together anymore."

"Wasn't it lonely?"

"At the time, I didn't grasp the concept of loneliness."

"But that's changed now that you've met people. Made friends."

"Friends?" she almost sputtered. "I have no friends."

"Hello, me." Babette waved.

"How did we become friends?" was her incredulous query.

"Well, you haven't tried to kill me. We've shared food. You told me about the great sex you had with your lover. In my book, that's the start of a great friendship."

"Maalik is not my lover."

"Fuck buddy then. After all, not everyone wants to have the whole love thing involved."

"Jinn don't love."

"Do you date?"

She shook her head.

"Marry?"

Another negative.

"Then how do you make baby genies?"

"We don't. There are only a finite amount of us."

"Well shit. That makes you rare, then. Possibly even endangered, given you can be killed now."

Daava's lips pursed. "Your reminder isn't very friendly."

Babette hugged her. "Fear not, little genie. I

won't let anyone take you out unless you're bad. Even then, depends on the crime. I'm not averse to a little mayhem, if you know what I mean." Babette winked.

It brought a smile. "You are strange. But I am enjoying your company."

"Ditto. Which is why it's such a shame you're into the walking muscle factory. Although, if you're going to be into guys, at least you chose a pretty one."

"He is attractive. I believe I will miss him."

"Your guy is not gone yet," Babette pointed out.

"But he shall depart shortly." The question being, would he return? Was this goodbye?

I don't want him to go. But how could she get him to stay?

"If you don't want him to leave, then stop him. It's what I would do." Babette's suggestion intrigued.

"How? Chains? I wonder if they would be hard to conjure. I'd need a proper bed, too. This one lacks posts," Daava mused aloud, eyeing it.

"While I like the way your mind works, not sure he'd appreciate you taking him hostage. Unless you're also planning seduction."

Touch him as he'd touched her? He'd made it clear he no longer had an interest. "I do not think that will work. He's found what he wanted." And it wasn't her.

"Has he? He didn't look overjoyed if you ask me."

Nice to see her initial assessment confirmed, and yet, that didn't change the fact he immediately sought directions to find Ellona. "Maalik isn't one to turn from a chosen path." He'd chased down the Shaitan with single-minded abandon.

"Maybe he wouldn't be so keen if you hexed her. Give her a few extra tails or bad breath."

Render Ellona unattractive? It had possibility. "I once gave an old master a second manhood."

"How is that bad? Isn't that every guy's fantasy?"

"On his forehead."

Babette's jaw dropped. "That. Is. Epic. Can you do something like that to Ellona?"

The insistence made Daava frown. "I am surprised you'd think it appropriate. She is a dragon."

"Not family. Not a friend. Besides, whatever you do can be temporary, right?"

A time limit could be placed or terms to break a curse. One thing held her back, though. "Maalik will be angered if I harm the one he loves."

"Probably, but would you really notice? The

man scowls all the time. Maybe we should be thankful he has his girlfriend back. He might not need the rest of his wishes."

"Doubtful. People are never happy with what they have." That oasis was nicer than this one. His camel fiercer. His wife prettier. Even those that thought they were doing good caused more harm.

I want peace for my village. The flood took care of the fighting.

I want my family to be happy. Said by a poor man who thought himself so clever not asking for riches. He died, run over by an out-of-control camel. The owner, contrite, gave the family enough wealth to leave their patch of arid land and move to the city where the wife remarried a merchant and lived in a lovely home. The sons took on a trade. The daughters made good marriages. And the family was happy.

"Don't you worry, little genie. We'll make sure he doesn't do anything stupid with his remaining wishes." Babette patted her hand as if the gesture could actually do anything. It did oddly enough. It soothed Daava. "Once the guy is done with the wishes, we'll find a way for you to live free."

"You'd do that?" The idea terrified and elated.

"That's what friends do." Babette hugged

Daava close once more just as Jeebrelle entered the room, wearing her satchel around her torso.

"Is everything okay?" asked the plague mage with a frown.

"Peachy, eh, little genie?" Babette kept her arm around Daava.

"We are friends," Daava announced, basking in the concept.

"What has the Shaitan done to you?" Jeebrelle's gaze narrowed. "Has she placed you under a spell?"

"Like she said, we're friends, Jeebs. Like me and you. Nothing more. Just. Friends." For some reason, Babette appeared to be pointed about this.

Jeebrelle glanced away. "We need to leave. Maalik senses a coming peril."

"Ooh. Really?" Babette crooned. "Should I change?" She glanced at her outfit.

"We must go." Maalik appeared behind Jeebrelle, and a jolt of awareness hit Daava as their gazes met.

His warning came too late.

Chapter Fourteen

Crash. Glass tinkled as something broke through the window and tangled in the fabric covering it.

"What the ever-loving fuck?" Babette exclaimed. She didn't retreat but strode for the curtain and yanked it back, revealing a beetlelike creature, slightly larger than a cat, with a hard carapace. "What is that?"

"Sand beetle," Daava declared. "And where there's one…" Her statement fizzled as a glance at the window showed more of them arriving.

"Are they dangerous?" Babette asked, avoiding the clacking mandibles.

"Not really, but they can be a nuisance," Maalik declared, moving from the doorway. No surprise, he scowled at the approaching scuttle of bugs.

"How are they here?" Jeebrelle asked. "They aren't native to this continent."

"They're a tool of the Shaitan." His glance met Daava's.

"It wasn't me," she felt a need to declare as she backed with Babette toward the door to the hall where Jeebrelle stood, her hand on the knob.

"If not you, then who?" Maalik barked.

"Does it matter?" Babette asked as Jeebrelle opened their exit.

"It does because if it's not her—"

"The Shaitan have obviously found us. We have to go." Jeebrelle huffed.

"How could they have found us, though?" Maalik asked. Only to turn his gaze on Daava, once more accusing. "You contacted them."

"No."

"Then who? Because it wasn't me or Jeebrelle."

"Not me, either!" Babette protested as they spilled into the hall.

Indignation had Daava exclaiming, "I didn't contact anyone."

"Sure, you didn't." Maalik headed for the moving box they called an elevator and jabbed the button on the wall, making it illuminate.

Leaning on the wall, Babette eyed the empty

corridor they'd just traversed. "How dangerous are those beetles?"

"More a nuisance than anything else. They will sting and cause welts to flesh, but they've never been known to kill." Jeebrelle appeared serene, standing in a flowing caftan from which peeked her toes wearing sandals.

Daava's feet and legs were bare. She'd not fully dressed before they departed. Then again, neither had Maalik.

"If they're mostly harmless, why send them?" Babette mused. "They were way too easy to escape."

"We haven't escaped yet," Daava reminded. She eyed the glowing red symbols above the elevator door that kept changing, indicating its approach. Such a marvelous world thus far. Perhaps skipping three thousand years would turn out to be a positive.

"The bugs pushed us into the hall, which means whoever sent them wanted that to happen," Babette remarked.

"What do your visions say?" Jeebrelle turned to Maalik for an answer.

He shook his head. "This time, this place, there is so much static. It's hard to see."

"Forget getting trapped in the elevator. We're getting out another way." Babette led the charge to the far end of the hall and another door. Upon opening it, Daava spotted stairs.

Her turn to pause.

Maalik noticed. "What's wrong?"

She glanced at him. "This feels like a trap."

His brow furrowed as he sought to see. He growled in frustration. "And I can't see, meaning whatever happens next involves me."

"If little genie's guts say it's a trap, then it's a trap." Babette eyed the hallway then suggested a tad eagerly, "We should find a good spot to stand our ground and fight."

"You can't fight the Shaitan, not without the killing stave," Jeebrelle remarked.

"Not to mention, we can't let them steal Daava. There must be a direction we can use to escape." He closed his eyes, grimacing until Daava remarked, "Is your stomach paining you?

"No. I'm trying to see."

"I agree with Daava. Looks like you're having a shit. And it's taking too long. I say we go this way." Babette turned and kicked open a door, which led to screams and threats.

Humans. Always prone to theatrics. They also

liked to argue against bad odds. A man wearing a robe and nothing else blustered, "Get out or I'm calling security."

"You are the one who needs to leave," Maalik growled.

The human puffed out his chest. "Now listen here—"

Daava waved her hand to silence him and his screaming companion still in the bed, holding the covers to her bare bosom. "You heard the mage. Depart at once." To hurry them along, Daava set fire to the bed. The humans fled the room, while Maalik flung magic at the window, shattering it.

"You know, you could have just opened it. Now we gotta watch for glass," Babette complained as she clambered through. A glance showed her standing on a section of pebbly roof jutting from the main part of the hotel, and home to many noisy and belching metal chimneys.

Soon all four of them were on the roof, and the beetles—still streaming into a window that must be theirs—noticed. They changed direction, pouring from the top of the hotel, roiling down the side in a wave.

"That's a lot of beetles to squish. Time to bug out," Babette declared before she changed into a dragon.

Jeebrelle, though, rather than shift, chose to climb atop the silver. When Maalik flipped into his other form, Daava realized their plan was to fly away. Why not portal?

Maalik bugled and lowered his head. A clear demand she climb him.

"That seems dangerous." She, who used to fly carpets, racing any who dared challenge. That was before she had a squishy body. Given how much it hurt when she butted her toe on the wall, she didn't want to know what a full body would feel if it landed on the ground from a great height.

Clack. Click. A glance behind showed the beetles arriving, also a painful prospect, but more worrisome, overhead was a gathering storm of dark clouds. In that roiling mass, a presence that pushed at her.

She shoved right back.

A voice with no sound spoke to her. *Why do they reject us?*

Because she didn't want to be an us. She wanted to stay a me, and that meant escaping the Shaitan collective.

Daava ran for the dragon, reaching for the scales at his shoulders as she climbed on. It wasn't easy to position herself. The scales were more abrasive than her skin liked, which was why, as people emerged from the hotel and pointed from the pavement below, she used her magic to steal their clothes. Some to wear, like the scarf for her neck and socks for her feet, but more of it to use as layers for a saddle held in place by magic. The same magic that kept her from falling off when Maalik leapt from the building. He soared, his massive wings snapping out, spreading to gather the breezes and then using them to push higher and higher.

Their escape didn't go unchallenged.

Return at once.

The imperious demand had her putting hands to her ears as if that would stop the voice.

She projected a single thought. *No.*

The refusal was met with a fireball that only barely missed as Maalik tilted to avoid its passage. A peek behind showed more coming.

She did her best to counter. However, as she'd noticed since her return, either something plagued her abilities, or magic had changed.

A good thing Maalik could fly. He might be massive in shape, yet he moved adeptly, rolling and diving, avoiding the missiles. Bugling a challenge in his dragon voice.

She'd have sworn he said, "Do something."

Like what? Shaitan didn't fight each other. They merged. She didn't want that.

Maalik aimed upward for the gray bank of clouds, pumping his wings and arrowing through the sky. Fast. So fast. Soon they were through the clouds and coasting over them.

There was sunshine. So much of it Daava squinted, but even then, her eyes teared. Ew. And to think humans indulged in crying at almost anything.

The scarf she'd acquired was wrapped around her head, shielding her eyes a bit, but it took goggles of air, basically magical shields, to properly see.

A silver dragon swooped close, Jeebrelle's hair streaming as she held on with just her knees. Her mouth opened, and she spoke, but Daava heard nothing. Jeebrelle pointed behind.

Sure enough, the Shaitan had followed. Only one of them. It chased them on his carpet, a shadowy blob that managed to remain dark despite the bright sunshine. It had given up trying to convince Daava to join it and now simply oozed menace.

Jeebrelle uttered a piercing whistle to draw attention. Babette aimed for the portal that formed.

Escape. The only way to rid themselves of the Shaitan.

Maalik bellowed in reply, and the dragons

began to weave, the silver surging ahead to the portal Jeebrelle had created, which meant they missed Maalik veering. A different portal appeared and swallowed them.

Chapter Fifteen

The portal Maalik created took them to a lake he'd recently been using as a camp. It was nestled in a valley. Not a place easily stumbled upon. A quiet haven to regroup and figure out what to do. Because suddenly it didn't seem so clear.

He had to speak with Ellona. Of that there was no question. But what to do with Daava? He'd planned to leave her in the care of Jeebrelle, who, unlike Israfil, wouldn't kill her out of hand. The attack of the Shaitan had changed everything.

For one, it showed they still wanted Daava. Why? They couldn't free the Iblis anymore. Or could they? Best not to find out, which meant he couldn't leave Daava unprotected. So how then could he speak with Ellona?

Argh. The annoyed bellow emerged as he landed.

Rather than dismount, Daava remained on his back with questions. "Where are the others?"

As if he knew. Portals didn't display addresses.

She answered as if she'd heard a reply. "Why did you take us somewhere else? We were supposed to follow them."

Supposed to. *Ha.* It emerged as a snort.

"Babette will be angry with you."

He yawned. As if he cared what a lesser dragon thought.

"I should be cross with you."

Cross? After he'd rescued her from the Shaitan? Or did she consider that a bad thing? Perhaps she wanted to be reunited with the others.

"You are difficult to understand." The heavy sigh at the end had him shifting.

"*I'm* difficult?" He managed indignity, despite the fact he lay under her.

She remained straddling him and leaned down. "Yes, you are."

"Says the cryptic one in this duo." His casual words belied his state of readiness. He caught her off guard when he flipped them around so she lay on her back with him squashing her.

Her eyes rounded, but her lips curved. "Are you

about to give me more lessons in the way fornication can be pleasant?"

"No." But lying atop her body, the rest of him wasn't as sure.

"Are you certain? Because you feel ready to stab me." She wiggled under him and proved correct.

He was hard. Ready. Willing and wanting. But what of Ellona? If he wanted a chance with her…

"I am not having sex with you."

"Why not?" She actually pouted.

He wanted to kiss it from her lips. "Because of what just happened."

"We escaped. It is cause for celebration. Yes?" She sounded so cutely optimistic.

The temptation proved real. He shook his head. "No celebration. Rather, concern about that targeted attack."

"It was to be expected the Jinn would come for me."

"Why? With one of the Shaitan gone, you don't have enough combined magic to bring the Iblis over."

"Are you sure they're gone?"

He wanted to say yes, and yet… If he took a second to peek, he could see a future where the Iblis found a way to ravage the earth. A frown tugged his features. "The weapon exists. I've seen it. Seen what it can do."

The claim lifted her shoulders. "And I know our kind isn't so easily rid of. Could be the stave merely dispersed the Shaitan. Perhaps it can reform."

He growled. "Is that what happened? Tell me."

"Is that a request, Master?"

The term was a good reminder he dealt with a trickster. "No. People can converse without everything they say being construed as a wish."

"And yet, you are not most people because you and I have a bargain that I must fulfill."

The reminder was one to watch his tongue. "When I want a wish, I will specify I am using it. Right now, I want answers to my question. Did you betray our location?"

"No."

"Are you speaking to the others?"

"There is no speaking with them."

"How do I know you're not lying?"

"You don't."

Call it instinct, but he got the impression she spoke the truth. "You asked why I ditched Jeebrelle and her lackey."

"To get us some private time for sex." Only her impish smile let him know she teased.

"If you didn't contact the other Jinn, then how

were we found? Only two others knew of our location. Jeebrelle wouldn't betray us like that."

Her turn to have a crease on her brow. "Nor would Babette. On the contrary, she said she'd try and find a way for me to be free of the bargain."

"How? She doesn't have magic," he scoffed.

"There are times I wish I didn't either."

The very real longing in her tone struck him. Daava might actually mean it. A Jinn who didn't want to be a Jinn. Not long ago the very concept would have been unfathomable.

"Is it possible to rewrite the bargain your kind made?" he asked.

"I don't know. But it would be nice to try."

"And you think a dragon you just met is the solution."

"Babette is my friend."

He snorted. "By what measure?"

"Unlike you, she never tried to stuff me into a ring."

He wouldn't apologize. "I didn't technically harm you."

She snorted.

How could a Shaitan snort in amusement? Then again, how could one come on his fingers?

"Harm is for me to decide, not you. And it's too

soon to tell what you will do to me because you still have two wishes."

"I won't hurt you with them. I promise." He also meant it.

"I guess you've already gotten the biggest thing you asked for. The one you love has returned." Spoken sourly, almost as if jealous.

"Did you return Ellona? Given your lack of knowledge about it, I am thinking you didn't actually have to do anything to accomplish that." Had Ellona been alive this entire time?

"Doesn't matter what I did or didn't do. Your wish came true. You're welcome."

He should be thankful, and yet he found himself more irritated than ever. "Ellona's back, but that's only the beginning. The last time we saw each other, she wasn't happy with me." Understatement. She'd tried to choke him, only her hands weren't big enough to wrap around his neck.

"Angry women are easy. Get her a pretty bauble. More than a few wishes I've granted involved jewelry to please a wife or mistress. Perhaps something for her hoard?"

"I doubt there's anything material I could give her that would assuage her temper."

"Then how will you gain her forgiveness?"

"I thought I'd start with an apology."

She stared at him long and quiet enough he squirmed. Almost uttered a revealing groan as he found himself discomfited.

"What?" he finally snapped.

"I might not have had a body and emotions as long as you, but even I know words are rarely enough."

"They're just the start," he defended.

"How long has Ellona been angry with you?"

"A while," he hedged.

She arched a brow. "I'm confused. I thought you were in love."

"We are. Were. Will be," he added. "Our relationship became stressed by our forced proximity. Things got tense. She was especially upset as she perceived I lied to her."

"Did you?"

"More like omitted some details of what I'd seen."

"She was angry."

"Very."

"And she left?"

"A few times, but she always came back, which is why I never suspected she might have faked her death."

"That doesn't sound like love." A stark statement he didn't want to examine because it would throw thousands of years into disarray.

He shifted uncomfortably. "It's complicated."

"You could untangle it with a wish."

The suggestion caused him to bark in laughter. "Let me guess, you will uncomplicate things by killing her."

"Or you, because, apparently, her previous death didn't resolve the issue."

"How about no one dies?"

"It would be the simplest solution."

"Only for you. I don't know what the answer is to my problem, but I do know we both have to be alive if I'm going to win her back."

"And if she doesn't want you? Or you no longer want her?"

"Then I'll—" He'd what? His only focus thus far had been to get Ellona to forgive him and love him again. What if it didn't happen? What then?

It was Daava who dared speak it aloud. "Did it ever occur to you perhaps you're meant to love someone else?"

"No." Then again, for three thousand years he'd only really thought of one woman, which, in hindsight, might have been due to his restricted options. But circumstances had changed. He had the choice to find another, but then again, now that they weren't trapped, the problems that had plagued him and Ellona were gone as well.

"It seems to me emotions are chaos. I don't know why anyone indulges in them." Daava's nose scrunched.

"Are you going to tell me you're not enjoying feeling?" Because he'd seen her wonderment as she discovered the pleasures of the senses.

"I do like it. However, I imagine it is only a temporary thing because of this body."

He was good. He didn't ogle said body. "Do you want to go back to being a smoky menace?"

She shrugged. "It is what I am."

"Would you prefer remaining flesh?"

"Yes, but that's impossible."

"Can't you wish for it?"

"A Jinn cannot make a wish. We can only do minor magics on our own."

"Meaning someone else could ask for it to happen."

"Why, Maalik, are you going to make me your flesh slave?" she asked sweetly, yet it angered.

"You're not my slave."

"May I leave?"

"No!" he practically barked.

"As you command, Master." She bowed her head, and he saw how she'd trapped him.

"You're not a slave. I won't hurt you."

"No, but you will override my wishes if they don't coincide with yours because you plan to use me. Which is fine. You released me, and the bargain says I owe you wishes. But don't blame me if the result isn't what you expected." Her tone emerged dull.

"Meaning what? That you'll twist my intent?"

"Have you fully thought through what you want? The consequences if you get it?"

"What kind of consequences? It's simple. I want Ellona to love me again. Make that my wish." He almost bit his tongue as he said it.

The statement caused Daava to shake her head. "You might want to think about that. We can compel attraction, however, true love? The kind that resonates in the soul? That's not something any wish can do."

"But you admit you can force desire?" The revelation had him shouting, "You're using magic to make me want you."

Her face was almost comical with surprise. "Why would I do that?"

Why indeed, when he knew for a fact she'd not experienced desire before. Why would she suddenly demand it?

"My attraction for you isn't natural," he argued.

"Whatever you feel, it's not magic."

"Says you."

"I am starting to see why being with you is difficult," she muttered. She glanced at her stomach. "It's making noise again."

"You're hungry." And so was he, but not just for food. Daava still wore only a skimpy shirt, meaning much of her legs were exposed. He knew for a fact there was nothing more underneath.

"Can we get some of those delicious things we ate before?" She clapped her hands and bounced.

The enthusiasm confused, especially since he had an intense desire to please.

He raked fingers through his hair. "You'll have to make do with what I forage from the forest." Because he didn't dare portal into town and leave her alone.

"You are going to hunt? That will take time. Don't you have an abode nearby with supplies?"

"No house. Just what you see around us."

She glanced left, right, behind, and shook her head. "That won't do. I would like a hot shower and to rest on that soft bed again."

"Sorry, but I can't—"

She snapped her fingers.

A mattress with sheets—the same as the hotel they just left—landed on a flat spot, then the chair and divan. The shower walls and spouting water head didn't survive the trip, but the tub did. Although it did cause a momentary frown on Daava's face before she once more clicked her digits. Water from the lake poured into the tub and began to steam.

She smiled. "I think I shall enjoy my first bath."

Daava stripped out of her clothes. Her shorter hairstyle meant he could see every delectable curve. He remembered her coming on his fingers.

His cock hardened, knowing how good it would feel to be sheathed when she climaxed. He had a gut feeling Daava wouldn't say no. But then again, she wasn't exactly free to say yes. Would she if she had the choice?

Didn't matter. Not now that he had a chance to make amends with Ellona.

What if, now that their imprisonment was over, she didn't hate him? What if he could apologize and they started over?

He stared a moment longer, for some reason torturing himself, before he walked away.

Chapter Sixteen

Woe is me. Bored. So bored.

Babette sighed and wondered how to turn her doldrums into fundrums. It had been a day since they'd lost Maalik and the little genie. Once Jeebrelle realized they wouldn't be easily found, she'd left to do whatever a horsewoman of the apocalypse did when she wasn't plaguing Babette with dirty thoughts.

Does she, or doesn't she? The burning question. Babette sure as hell did. Want Jeebrelle, that was. Loved and wanted that woman like she'd never wanted another. Despite this, her brashness suddenly failed her. Where Jeebs was concerned, she tiptoed around her attraction.

What if she misread the vibes? What if she ruined their burgeoning friendship?

The frustration left her throwing darts at a cat that hissed and batted them away before they even came close. Feisty thing. It would make a nice snack later so long as its horseman didn't find out. Israfil appeared attached to the mangy thing.

Elspeth suddenly stood in her line of fire yet somehow pulled a Matrix and managed to avoid getting hit by darts.

"Damn, look at you move." She flung the final one, only to have Elspeth lean over and pluck it midair before it could connect with the feline.

"No poking the cat."

"Ah, why did you have to ruin my fun?" Babette grumbled as the critter turned, lifted her tail, farted, then left.

"Had you actually managed to hit the cat and eat it, the Silvergrace family would have gone to war against the dragon mage who owns it, as he would have retaliated."

That led to a most pressing question. "Would we have won the war?"

"Nope."

"In that case, it's a good thing you're here."

"I planned it that way." Elspeth beamed.

"At least you're good at predicting the future. I hung out with another seer recently, and he was shit at it."

"I'm so jealous you met the renowned Maalik." Elspeth clasped her hands. "Is he as wise as they say?"

"Who says?"

"The voices in one of the future forks. They're quite enamored by him."

"And the other paths?"

With a nonchalant wave, Elspeth said, "I'm sure most of those won't come to pass."

Eep.

"Is there a reason you've escaped your keeper?" Babette asked, eyeing Elspeth as she waddled past with her baby belly. Given who the daddy was, people wagered on it emerging with horns and a tail.

Babette put her money on Luc passing out in the delivery room when he found out it was twins. Because, hello, she'd noticed Ellie's nursery with the oversized crib and the bountiful amount of unisex clothing. Enough for two. Given Luc's overprotective nature now, no wonder Elspeth kept that part secret.

"I'm here to say excellent work, best friend. Everything is going splendidly."

"How do you figure that?" Babette growled. "I lost the genie and the fifth horseman, who doesn't have a horse, by the way."

"Which is as it should be. Maalik and Daava must figure things out on their own."

"That's scary given they're both morons."

"I know. They're perfect for each other." Elspeth sighed and wore a sappy expression.

"Speaking of perfect, I don't suppose you see something hot and sexy in the future for me."

The pat on Babette's hand didn't reassure. "Patience. I promise, the wait will be worth it."

"I hate waiting."

"Good thing you have plenty to keep you busy while you do. Which reminds me, your mother sent me to fetch you. Apparently, she's got a lovely young woman she'd like you to meet."

"What? No. Hell no."

Mother had decided it was time Babette settled down. It began with her sending Babette images of wedding tuxedos with flaring skirts. A stronger hint was the fact she'd also begun trying to set Babette up with all her friends' daughters and nieces.

Annoying. Babette would marry when the right woman came along—say like the one who came riding into the world on a pale horse.

Chapter Seventeen

Ah, this is nice.

Daava lounged in her outdoor tub, sporadically reheating the water, until her skin wrinkled. She only rose from it when Maalik emerged from the woods carrying his finds. There might have been some calculation at her timing. After all, ignorant in some things didn't mean completely oblivious when it came to others.

"How was your hunt?" she asked, cocking a hip.

He gaped at her wet body. It gave rise to that tingle between her legs. A tingle he knew how to handle.

"I see you managed to forage. Rabbit. Berries and…" Her nose wrinkled. "Weeds?"

He rehinged his jaw enough to mumble, "Dandelion leaves. For a salad."

It didn't look very appetizing, but to her surprise, without the use of magic, Maalik managed to create a rather edible meal. He cooked the meat —liberally sprinkled with seasonings he'd stashed in a crevice of rocks —over a fire he built.

"That was quite palatable," she grudgingly admitted. "I especially liked the crackly juicy parts."

"The fire crisps the fat nicely."

Who would have thought she'd ever eat animal flesh and like it? Even the weeds provided an interesting culinary delight.

He kept introducing her to new and pleasurable things, so was it any wonder that when she saw Maalik leave their meal spot to run and leap in the lake, she thought, what was the harm in following?

She did exactly as he did. Jumped in. And sank. The bottom took a while to hit, and when she did, she panicked. For one, she couldn't see, and her chest was tight. She wanted to breathe but even she knew better than to inhale water.

I must swim. Easy to think, harder to do. Moving her arms and legs did nothing. Her lungs hurt with the ache of holding in her air. A glance overhead showed the lighter surface. So close. Her magic slipped away, the water dispersing it before she could properly grasp it.

Her vision had begun to fade when something

grabbed hold of her arm and pulled at her, tugged her until her head broke the surface and she could take a deep breath.

"You idiot," Maalik exclaimed. "You could have drowned!"

He was angry, and yet she beamed. "You saved me." She knew enough of how things worked in the world to realize that deserved a kiss.

She pressed her mouth to his, caught his gasp of surprise. The embrace lasted a few flesh-heating moments before he pulled away.

"No. We can't." He said it, and yet she sensed his arousal. Should she prove him wrong and show him they could?

It reminded her of the masters she'd had who thought they could cajole her into being receptive to their advances. The comparison didn't sit well. She kept her lips to herself.

"Can you return me to shore? My magic isn't working at all in this water."

As he towed her to shore, he said, "Is it just me, or did you notice a difference in power levels for this era?"

"It feels different." The magic reacted differently, too. As if something within it had shifted but she'd attributed it to her new body.

"I think it's still changing."

"Is that important?" she asked.

"I don't know yet."

The deep water suddenly turned shallow and she could stand. He'd yet to release her, though. As they slogged to the grassy area holding their bed, she stripped off her sodden clothes.

It caused him to suck in a breath. "What are you doing?"

"It's wet.

"So dry it."

A glance at him showed he'd used some magic to sluice his garments.

She quirked a corner of her lip. "Isn't that a waste of your power when it will dry overnight?" She tossed the wet mess onto a rock and moved to the bed.

"I don't suppose you could conjure a second mattress?"

"Is that a wish, Master?" she deliberately teased.

"No. It just looks comfortable."

"We already know it's big enough for both of us." She snuggled under the sheets, leaving him room on the other side.

Still, he hesitated. "I should keep watch."

She yawned. "I know you already set some wards to warn us if anyone, friend or foe, approaches."

"I really should—"

She tired of his excuses, especially since a sudden insight gave her the cause. "Are you afraid to share this bed?" Because, while innocent about some things, she recognized a man nervous about something.

"No."

"Then come."

He didn't reply, but he did move to the far side of the mattress and lay atop the covers on the far edge.

She inwardly smiled. For a man in love with another, he appeared torn. Oddly enough, it pleased her, as did the dream she fell into.

A dream with Maalik doing more touching and kissing. It shouldn't have been a surprise to wake up cradled in his arms, that wet, tingling feeling between her legs again.

But if she'd hoped for a repeat with his hand, bringing her pleasure…

He scrambled from the bed as if set on fire. "I'll go see if I can find us any berries for breakfast."

Frustration had her staring at the sky, the dawn sun just rising. She sighed. The throb between her legs was still insistent. She thought of the times she'd come across humans touching themselves. Could she pleasure herself?

Her hand slid down to the vee between her thighs. Her finger explored the nether lips, and the moisture between, but when she found her pleasure button and rubbed? She managed with some clumsy fumbling to give herself an orgasm.

Chapter Eighteen

Maalik woke, hard and willing. He'd enjoyed such pleasant dreams. Erotic ones involving the woman cradled against his body. It would be so easy, and pleasurable, to take what she offered, until he reminded himself what he'd be giving up if he did.

Think of Ellona.

Guilt hit him hard, and he practically ran from the bed. As he bolted for the woods, he yelled, "I need a private moment."

He ran hard enough his chest heaved for air. Only then did he pause that he might take a few deep breaths to calm down. He took time to glare at his cock, too. It remained semi hard despite the chill morning air. It didn't care that Daava wasn't the one that should be giving it a rise. A dragon his age should better control his primal urges.

Tell that to the man starved for sexual attention. He'd have to do something about it. But not with Daava. He'd fix things with Ellona and soon all his carnal needs would be handled. If not, he and his hand were well acquainted.

He took in a few more breaths and, when he had himself in check, headed back for the camp. What a reckless thing for him to do, fleeing with barely a word. Alone, who knew what kind of mischief Daava would get into? The wards he'd set the previous day only served to let him know if anyone tried to enter—or leave. They wouldn't tell him what she did while he was gone.

Did she circumvent his defense? Contact the other Jinn? Miss him? Think of him? Touch herself while thinking of him?

Why couldn't he stop fantasizing about her? She was Shaitan. He couldn't trust her because he couldn't forget she was a monster…with thoughts and feelings expressed in words that showed him a different perspective. Made him question so much.

Including his obsession with Ellona.

Did he love her? He certainly had at one time, and when he thought her dead, he'd spent all his time reflecting on their time together. Over and over. He had nothing else to do. It kept him from going crazy.

But that didn't make obsession with Ellona healthy.

The thought stuck with him as he returned more slowly through the woods. His steps were quiet in case he hadn't scared off all the potential breakfast in the area. Being quiet meant he heard her before he saw her. A soft moan that roused his protective instinct.

She's being hurt.

Being close to camp, he chose stealth over speed that he might perceive the situation before charging in. A good thing, too. He managed to slow in time to avoid interrupting Daava.

Who was masturbating.

He wavered on his feet. *Turn away. Don't watch.* He couldn't avert his gaze. It was wrong to intrude on her moment. Then again, she'd been more than blunt with her desire for him.

Would she want him to watch as she stroked herself?

Yes. Or so he hoped. He was mesmerized by the hand moving between her legs.

What did it mean that he burned with jealousy that her own fingers touched instead of him? If he moved into view, announced his presence, would she invite him to sink between her thighs? Thrust into her with his cock? Feel the ripples of her climax?

The hand on his cock moved at the same pace as her fingers on her body. He stroked in time, driven by her soft cries, and when her head turned to the side, he'd have sworn she looked right at him. Her lips certainly moved, shaping his name.

Maalik.

He couldn't have said who came first, only that he spurted as she cried out and arched. When he was done, he leaned against a tree and closed his eyes.

So much for control. He should feel shame. After all, not only had he been a peeper, he'd once more betrayed Ellona.

However, it wasn't what he'd done that left the pit of dread in his stomach. Knowing he'd soon see Ellona again caused that.

Where was the joy? The exhilaration?

Just nerves. Once he saw her and they spoke, he'd—

He had no idea what would happen because he couldn't see his future or Ellona's. Until now, he'd not seen Daava either, but as he wiped himself clean with magic, he received a single clear vision. Daava, a soft serene smile on her lips and, still in the flesh, cradling a child with chubby cheeks, flailing fists, and curly hair in her arms.

Whose baby was it? Daava had said herself Jinn didn't procreate. They were entities more spirit than anything. The Daava in the vision wasn't smoke though, and neither was the baby. Could it be hers?

If so, who fathered it?

Puzzled and oddly annoyed, Maalik made much noise as he emerged from the woods. Did she scramble to hide her antics?

Nope.

She basked in the dawn sun atop the sheets, wearing only a smug smile.

"Did you bring back any food?" she asked, her gaze going to his hands by his sides.

Logically he knew that was what she eyed, but his cock? He thought she looked at it, and it started to swell again.

Maybe she wouldn't notice. He made hand gestures to draw her attention away. "No, and I don't have time to forage. I'll go to town to fetch some."

"Ooh. Shopping. The masters' wives used to make much ado about that particular pastime." She scrambled to her feet and bounced on the mattress in a most distracting manner.

Breasts up. Jiggle down. The nipples pert

berries that would have made him a perfectly fine break of his overnight fast.

"You can't come," he stated more harshly than deserved.

Her grin never faltered once as she smartly replied, "I just did. Turns out you're not the only one who can bring pleasure to my body."

Was it wrong to want to yell that he did it better? He wanted so badly to prove that he could make her come harder and more intensely. At the same time, he couldn't believe how she'd twisted his words.

It was quite naughty of her. Clever, too. And yes, his cock enjoyed it as well.

Bad. He needed to get away and clear his head. "Can I trust you to not leave or contact the Shaitan while I fetch you food?"

"Stay here by myself?"

"I won't be gone long."

"Why can't I go then? How is it any more dangerous than leaving me here?"

"You could be spotted in town."

"Let's say I agree. What if you can't return? How long am I supposed to wait before I act?"

"I shouldn't be more than twenty minutes, thirty at the most." He knew a place that offered quick and delicious take-out.

"What if I'm attacked the moment you leave?"

"By what? A squirrel?"

"What's a squirrel? How does it taste?" She glanced at her stomach. "I'm hungry again."

"No one is watching us. I placed wards when I first started using this place."

"I can see why you like it. It's quite peaceful. No expectations. No demands. It would be perfect if it had a library and a restaurant that can make all the food."

"You just need a kitchen, and you could learn to cook it yourself."

"Like you did with our last meal. I will admit to being surprised at seeing a dragon mage doing the menial task of a lower caste."

"If there is one thing I learned during my imprisonment, it is that survival is more important than rank. What did you learn?" he hastily added.

"How to be just me. I'd like it to stay that way, too, please."

It was the please that did it. What if she was right and, the moment he left, the Shaitan swooped in?

"Very well, you can come. To town," he added in case she twisted it into something sexual again.

"Yay!" She clapped and bounced, her breasts a huge attraction.

He looked away. He could still see her body in his mind's eye, though.

"If you're coming, you need clothes. Head to toe. Shirt. Pants. Shoes." He ticked off the items, and she bit her lower lip.

"I have a shirt, but nothing for my legs or feet." She eyed them. Then him. "You don't either."

His grimace deepened. They'd left the hotel in a rush, only partially dressed. "I take it you still can't apparate stuff."

She shook her head. "Yesterday, I was only able to snatch a few things because I could see them."

"Does the same restriction apply to wishes?"

She bit her lower lip. "I don't know. The magic, as we've discussed, is different now."

What did that mean for his last two wishes? Maybe he should just ditch and forget them.

"We'll have to acquire some proper garments and footwear before we can move around town."

"Are the poor restricted to certain areas?" she asked.

"No, more like being barefoot has become taboo. If we don't wear shoes or boots, we will be noticed. Same with clothing. Humans don't seem to go about less than fully attired."

"Why? It is so nice to have one's skin exposed to

every sensation." She stretched and uttered a happy sigh.

"Think of it as preserving your enjoyment of nudity. How can you truly appreciate it unless you occasionally have to suffer wearing fabric?"

"It chafes." She pouted.

"Stay here then."

"I'll wear clothes if I must." Said with a forbearing sigh that almost made him smile.

He did grin when she had to wear her first shoes and complained.

"They're pinching my feet." She glared at the offending footwear, which he'd filched from an apartment that he entered via the roof access. He'd portaled them to a spot above it that he'd visited before.

"If you don't like them, toss on some magic to turn them into something more comfortable."

"Like dust?"

"Do you want to come with me for breakfast or not?" he said, trying to be stern, but she really was too cute in her disgruntlement over the shoes.

"Fine."

Her mannerisms continued to entertain him as they ate at the restaurant rather than taking the food to a park or alley. He paid with the plastic card he'd filched. How tapping it on a plastic box covered the expense, he didn't grasp, but it made everyone happy.

Only as they finished eating and emerged back onto the street did she ask, "Where to next?"

"We are going to locate Jeebrelle."

"Why? I thought you intentionally lost her."

"I did but now realize that might have been hasty, because I need her to keep an eye on you while I handle some business."

Daava's lips turned down as she stated, "You're leaving me."

Chapter Nineteen

There was no mistaking the sad expression on Daava's face. What was unexpected? How it almost undid Maalik. Especially since the last thing he actually wanted to do was leave. How had he come to care for his enemy? Was she even still his foe? Rather than planning her demise, he found himself wanting to kiss her.

The realization might have been why he injected more vehemence than necessary when saying, "You always knew my goal was to reunite with Ellona."

"I know. I just thought…" She trailed off before straightening to say, "I'll help."

He rejected her offer resoundingly. "No! I have to do this alone."

Again, the hurt on her face affected.

"Why can't I come with you?" Her voice was small.

The reasons he could list all boiled down to one major one.

"Because I don't know what to expect." The honest truth. Would Ellona kill Daava on sight? Given her anger issues, it actually seemed quite likely. Look at Israfil's reaction upon meeting Daava. Maalik had no doubt Israfil would have killed her if given a chance. "You'll be safer with Jeebrelle."

"Ha. This isn't about my safety. You're just worried you'll lose me before you get your wishes."

"It's not just about the wishes. Fuck the wishes." In that moment, he hated them. "It's more I don't know what to expect. Ellona can be a tad quick to act. It would be better if I met her alone first, which is why you'll stay with Jeebrelle."

"Why can't I return to our camp?"

"Because I worry what will happen if the Shaitan find you."

"That wouldn't be ideal," she admitted. "The Shaitan will force me to rejoin the collective."

"Which would be a shame."

"Especially if they did so before you collected your due," she grumbled.

"Actually, much as it pains me to admit, you're not a bad sort."

Her bad humor evaporated. "And you're not too horrible either, for a dragon mage." Her cheek dimpled as she smiled impishly.

Since when did she dimple? Why did he find it so adorable?

He glanced away. "Do you understand now why you need to be somewhere safe?"

"I'm safe with you."

The bald statement swelled his pride, but he remained a realist. "Usually I'd agree, but as mentioned, Ellona can react unpredictably. She might not react well to your presence."

"You think she will be jealous?" It might have been an innocent question but for Daava's knowing smirk.

"More like you're Shaitan, the enemy."

"You didn't touch me like the enemy."

The reminder heated his blood. "What happened with us was minor and before I knew of her return."

"You knew of her return when you watched me this morning."

"By accident," he protested. How much had she seen?

"What you were doing to your male parts didn't

look accidental," Daava remarked with a pointed glance at his groin.

He covered said groin with his hands. "Maybe what you saw was because I thought of Ellona."

That arched a brow. "Were you?"

He almost lied. It might have stopped this awkward conversation. "No. But it meant nothing. Men are carnal creatures. Visual ones, which means many things arouse us."

"I thought you were more than a man. What happened to your vaunted self-control?"

His lips flattened. "My control is fine."

"So I don't arouse you?" She stepped close and tilted her head, angling it enough he could have stolen a kiss.

"Stop it."

"Stop what?"

Stop making his heart race? Stop making him want to throw everything he'd planned away?

"Cease your attack on my actions."

"I am not attacking, merely pointing out an interesting fact. My understanding of love is that you should only desire Ellona."

There was a time that was true. He blamed their long absence from one another. "Once we are reunited—"

"Everything will be so perfect because you're so

in love." The mockery emerged lightly lilting but hit him hard, nonetheless.

His mood soured. Especially since he couldn't help but recall what Daava had said. What if the woman destined to be his lover wasn't Ellona but someone else?

Don't look at her. Don't look at— He glanced at Daava who'd pressed her face against a window. Her hands were flat on the glass as she ogled the display within.

"What is that statue wearing!"

A perusal indicated a garment of red straps and lace that covered nothing. He yanked her from the glass, even as it was too late. Daava would look incredible wearing it.

"I won't be dissuaded from finding Ellona," he muttered aloud, more to remind himself than Daava.

"Wasn't trying to. Just wanting to come along. I promise to remain out of sight. I'll wear a cloak as if I'm one of the dragon mages." She snapped her fingers, and suddenly she was swathed in a pale cloak of silky fabric.

"How did you do that? You claimed you couldn't conjure out of nothing."

"I can't. I saw this in a shop near the place we dined at."

"And thought you could just make it appear out of thin air? You can't do that," he rebuked her. "No magic where the humans can notice."

"No one saw," she insisted. "You put a spell on us to make everyone look away."

She'd noticed him doing that? And he thought himself so subtle. Yet, he had no choice given she drew attention. Especially from the males, who ogled her.

He fixed that.

"A good thing or you'd have been seen."

"Bah," she scoffed. "You worry overmuch. Humans think everything they see is superstitious or god based."

"The humans we used to know were gullible. Today's population is a bit more savvy. If they knew a Jinn actually existed, you'd be captured for study and hidden away."

"Does it involve a quiet cell with a bed and regular meals? Sounds good to me."

"Except I imagine you showing how you can grant wishes would be part of that studying. As might be dissecting." Or so he'd learned from the studies he'd done thus far of this era. Apparently, humans liked to take things apart—even people and animals—to see how they worked.

She grimaced. "That doesn't sound pleasant."

"Which is why you don't want to get caught."

For some reason this made her laugh. "Don't you think I've tried? Ever since the humans discovered the Jinn and began trapping us, we've been trying to find a way to break free of our curse. You don't know how many times I've wished I was more like you."

"Me?" He couldn't help a note of surprise.

"You're a dragon mage, one of the highest vaunted of your kind. Capable of wielding power. Serving yourself."

"And others," he hastily interrupted.

"But only if you want. You have the choice. And you are venerated."

"Not so much anymore."

"A temporary situation. Now that you and your brethren have returned, you will rise to the top again. I, however, will never be anything more than a hunted Jinn, whose consciousness could be shattered should I be broken into pieces again. And you wonder why I might want to be different?"

The response stuck with him, bothering him more than the upcoming meeting with Ellona, which neared with every beat of his wings.

They left the town and flew to the place called Toronto. Having memorized the map, he noted the landmarks on his path. The look-away spell kept him hidden from eyes in the sky. A very real threat. The humans could scry without magic, using drones and things called satellites. Eyes in space was how it was explained to him. Creepy and fascinating all at once.

Watching from his back, Daava exclaimed aloud over the many new sights. He'd had more time than her to immerse himself. Still, there remained a certain awe at some of the things he beheld.

"There are so many roads."

A network of them crisscrossing the continents all over the world. In their time, they never knew the world was so big. The oceans were too wide to fly across without rest. And why would they? Everyone of his era thought the world to be flat with the ocean spilling off its edge, taking those who strayed too far with it. But according to a book with many pictures and words he'd had to learn, the Earth was a ball, one of many spinning around the sun. There existed landmasses past the oceans. New places to discover. Knowledge to glean. Maalik had so many questions.

"There are so many chariots. Look at how rapidly they move. Where have they hidden the camels and horses?"

"Under the hood," a vagrant living under a bridge had told Maalik with a cackle.

False. Maalik had peeled back the odd material to find more machinery. Not beasts. The vehicles ran on combustion, an alchemical process that involved burning oil.

"Those buildings are so tall and straight. How is that possible?"

Because the world had moved on in their absence. The dragons, once at the peak, had fallen to humans, who, even now, were rolling faster and faster to their own golden age. When they failed, who would be next to rise? Dragons or someone else?

The knowledge brimming in this modern time daunted Maalik with just how little he, in fact, understood. He wanted to immerse himself in the history of how they'd gotten to this point. Maybe once he'd dealt with Ellona, he would.

It didn't seem prudent to fly directly to the tower Ellona had chosen as her perch. For all he knew, the Shaitan were watching Ellona, knowing of her link with Maalik. Then again, would they get close given she was one of their fiercest fighters?

The spell he'd cast to conceal their flight also covered them as they landed. He shifted into his man shape and felt more nervous than ever.

Daava, on the other hand, proved uncharacteristically quiet.

"Are you ill?" For she appeared pale.

"Fine. Getting hungry again, so let's hurry and find your lady love."

"I'll find her. Remember what I said about you remaining out of sight."

"I won't ruin your reunion. Promise."

He didn't know if he could believe her, but it proved the lesser of his problems. His instincts flared. A glance behind, overhead, showed no cause for alarm. Humans on the sidewalks ignored the man and woman walking, yet he couldn't shake the nagging sense someone watched and followed.

Their steps brought them eventually within sight of the distinctive spire he'd seen on the video. Spotting a place that served confectionaries and offered a place to sit inside, he entered. With his confiscated plastic card, he bought Daava some treats and placed her at a table out of view of the window.

She sat and eyed the food in front of her. "I smell sugar."

"Lots of it. Enough to keep you busy while I chat with Ellona."

"Only chat? I thought lovers who reunited after a long absence indulged in stabbing." Daava jabbed at something on the tray with a spoon.

He had no reply to that because she wasn't

wrong. He just couldn't see it happening. The closer he got to Ellona, the more he remembered their final fight.

"I can't believe you threw it away." It being the amulet, one of the seven seals, and the only one he'd brought with them in order to tie them to the spell. Break one, and their waiting period would end.

"Why do you care? It's not as if we can use it. Or were you planning to release the Shaitan within?"

She didn't reply.

His eyes widened. "Ellona, you can't!"

"Why not?" she yelled. "It would end this curse."

"But we fought so hard to contain them. Release one and it would all be for nothing."

"Would it, though? I'd get my life back."

A life without him in it. The novelty of being a couple had worn off quickly. Ellona wasn't the type to feel content with simply a home and hearth.

"I'm sorry you're unhappy."

"No, you're not, or you'd tell me where you hid the amulet."

"Somewhere no one will ever find it." He'd tossed it in the lake with its monster that guarded the bottom. A lake he'd later explored, only to discover it went deeper and farther than expected. So far, he wandered for a thousand years without running into anyone but creatures that wanted to eat him.

"I hate you," she'd screamed.

And then she tried to kill him.

The reminder didn't slow his step as he headed for the tower that drew a crowd. Everyone pointed and talked about the dragon that had chosen the spire for its roost.

The crowd thickened as he neared, making his passage difficult. In days long gone, humans would have bowed and never dared get in his way. Now? They barely spared him a glance, too busy with their little boxes that took pictures.

The reminder might have made the magical push to clear his path a bit rougher than needed, but it had an effect. It caused a ripple that split the gathered crowd apart enough to give him passage. He reached the cordon keeping the crowd from mobbing the base of the tower. Men in dark garb and helmets guarded the yellow rope.

As if that would stop him.

He walked right through it, magic shredding it to allow him passage. The men who approached he silenced, a temporary spell that forced them to look away while he dealt with his business.

For a man who'd cautioned subtlety, he flipped direction. He had no choice because the Ellona he knew wouldn't respect anything less than a show of strength.

Did the humans see? Let them. They'd never capture a dragon mage.

Maalik stood at the base of the tower and, for a moment, had a vision of it crumbled into chunks of debris, most of them scorched. A blink and he saw another future where it remained perfectly intact. Which one would become the true path? Would his actions today be the cause for the catastrophic version?

Too late to change his mind. The crowd wasn't the only one who noticed him.

Ellona bugled so loud the ground shook. Only a few of the smarter people scattered. Even more buzzed with excitement as more of the plastic boxes were aimed at him and angled to catch something overhead.

A glance upward showed Ellona leaned over the building's edge, her gaze fixed on him.

He waved.

He might as well have punched her.

Chapter Twenty

Y *OU!* Ellona's reply boomed in his head.

All hope for a happy reunion vanished, and Maalik realized in that moment how stupid he'd been to imagine any differently.

With a roar of irritation, Ellona dove off the tower and aimed for him.

Given she appeared as if she might actually unhinge her jaw wide enough to eat him, he decided to awe the ogling humans with his majestic self. Only…

His dragon wouldn't come. Try as he might, he remained locked in his two-legged form—which caused him a moment of panic because it reminded him of being trapped underground, adrift without magic or his true self.

The shock of being helpless hit him rapidly,

followed by annoyance at his own idiocy, which seemed to be doubling down. How had he not noticed the web of magic crisscrossing the area? The spell worked to suppress his dragon shape. Could he dismantle it?

No time to find out. With barely a second to spare, he dove to the side and Ellona swept past, a metal-scaled, raging dragoness who screeched in fury because he didn't stand still.

In the past, he'd allowed her to abuse him. Truly believed he deserved the slaps and punches. The old Maalik might have let her chomp him in half.

He wasn't that man anymore.

The mighty pumps of Ellona's wings took her high into the air. She hung overhead, a growling menace. The anger she displayed a sign she might not have changed much.

But, for the sake of their past, he tried. "I'm glad to see you've alive."

The rapid dive with claws extended indicated she didn't feel the same about him.

The strike took some swift footwork to evade. "Ellona! Stop. I just came to talk."

It appeared she wasn't interested in speaking, given she whirled around and tucked in tight for her next swoop.

"Dammit, why must you be so irritable all the time?" As he grumbled it, he questioned his decision in even coming here. Thousands of years and he remained dumb. Should have listened to his gut or, even better, not created some fantasy where he lived happily ever after with a woman who hated him. And quite honestly, how had he forgotten how little he liked her at times, too?

The problem now was extricating himself before his colossal stupidity killed him.

The dragoness landed, and her mouth opened wide as she sucked in a breath. He knew what would happen next, but the gawking humans didn't. They wouldn't be much of a loss on the procreation side given they lacked the common sense to run.

Ellona reached the apex of her inhalation, her chest as wide as it could get, readying to unleash her mighty breath.

A vision hit, hard and fast, flashing images. Ellona exhaling, killing everyone, perhaps even Maalik. He couldn't see himself, but he saw the humans hunting dragons. Systematically erasing all dragons, all shifters, all non-human life from the planet. All because a dragoness lost her temper.

Again.

"Calm down before you hurt someone, which will be—trust me—very, very bad."

An enraged Ellona didn't care. She exhaled in his direction, a grayish mist that rose and spread overhead, forming a cloud.

And the remaining crowd spent their last moments of life, faces tilted, watching.

Were they truly that oblivious? Just in case he could save a few, he yelled, "Run, you idiots, or you'll all die."

A few did. Too many didn't and stared slack jawed while pointing their devices.

The mist hardened, the cloud darkening before it dropped hundreds and hundreds of tiny metallic slivers that would impale flesh. Having been the recipient of it before, he could state with certainty it stung while in dragon shape. Those with human flesh? It would shred them.

"I am not dying today, Ellona." While he couldn't shift, the spell in the area didn't prevent him from using his innate power.

He drew magic from the air, the ground, all around him, and formed it into a barrier that covered him and spread overhead, protecting those he could reach. The invisible shield bounced the metal missiles, the ping of them almost musical until the screaming started by those still in the danger zone.

They didn't scream long. The missiles dissolved

almost immediately, and he dropped the shield. The last remaining humans finally fled. Except for one.

He held his plastic box on a stick and jumped around in excitement, speaking rapidly. Maalik had done enough warning. The idiot could die on his own anytime now.

Threat averted, he glared at Ellona, who landed and tucked her wings. She wove her head in Maalik's direction and hissed.

He didn't cower. "Do not start. Have you no honor left?"

"Grawr." The dragon blurred, and a woman appeared, wearing a toga in white and sandals with laces wrapped around her legs. As beautiful as ever, and yet, his blood didn't stir. "You would speak to me of honor?" Ellona cajoled.

"I'm not the one who faked my death."

Her hands exploded in motion. "What other choice did I have with you refusing to break that curse you placed me under?"

Again, with that argument. "I tried to dissuade you. You're the one who insisted on coming."

"Because I thought we'd actually be frozen in time. Go to sleep, wake up, and fight. That was what you promised. Instead, we lived no better than bugs underground, scrounging for everything. I was a queen reduced to nothing," she spat. "Stuck with the same people for an eternity."

"I didn't realize it would be for so long." On that he truly was being honest and sorry.

"You should have let me out."

"If I had, our sacrifice would have been for naught."

"It was for naught," Ellona yelled. "Look around you. You cursed us that we might return to save *humans*." She ended on a sneer.

"Not just humans. What of the dragons?"

She tossed her head. "The Septs of this time are weak. Which is also your fault."

"How is that my fault?" was his incredulous riposte.

"It's your fault the thirteen strongest of our time left instead of siring the next generation."

"Since when did you want children?"

Ellona had always firmly stated babies were not for her. A point of contention between them.

"Everyone wants an heir," she stated in a complete about-face.

"You didn't want one with me." He couldn't help but be bitter.

"Never you. If I am going to hatch a dragonling, it will be one that is guaranteed to be strong."

The implication didn't burn. On the contrary, being away from Ellona and everyone, alone, without even any visions for company, had shown him he did have strength. What he lacked, though, was her cruelty. He might be able to admit he didn't like how she treated him, yet, at the same time, he'd kept running back for more. Every time they were apart, he'd spent it plotting how to get her back.

No more. "You're right. I should have never let you join me. For that, I'm sorry."

"You will be." She stepped toward him, gaze cold and cruel.

To think he'd treated Daava like the enemy. So wrong. Maalik stood in front of a person who truly meant him harm. A woman he'd convinced himself into believing he needed. Always trying to atone for a supposed infraction. Always giving in to her will. Except for when it came to unraveling the spell.

She'd never believed him when he said he couldn't break it. Once cast, it had to run its course. One of the seven Shaitan seals had to be released. Which was why early on he'd dealt with the amulet used to tie them to the seals. Break it and the spell would collapse.

To avoid temptation, he rid himself of the amulet with its whispering voice inside.

After Ellona supposedly died, he spent forever trying to find it.

She raised her hand to slap him, and he caught her by the wrist. "No more hitting. Enough of the violence."

"Are you implying I'm abusive?"

"Actually, I'm saying it. You're mean, Ellona." Standing firm felt so liberating.

Finally, some surprise on her face. "Did you just call me mean? Is that how you're going to win me back?"

"I don't want you, Ellona." Not anymore. Never again.

"You're just saying that. We both know you are obsessed with me." She reached to touch him, and he leaned back.

"Don't. I mean it. I want nothing to do with you."

"Then why did you come here?"

"To prove something to myself. I deserve better."

"As if you could ever hope to have anything better than me, you clumsy oaf." A dragon of vision, he'd never been as adept as her when it came to fighting. He relied more on magic.

"You're right. I am clumsy. And dumb. Which is why you're better off without me."

Again, surprise lit her features, then an anger that hid swiftly under seductive words. "Oh, Maalik, we have reunited most terribly, haven't we?"

The sudden switch was familiar, but this time, without the blinders, he saw it. Saw the manipulation as she went from mean to sweet in an instant.

"Actually, this went about the same as usual. You mad about something and blaming me for it."

"Because you are at fault," she snapped.

"You know what? I don't actually care." He didn't. Didn't care she'd been missing. He finally understood why she'd faked her death. She didn't love him. Never had. If only he'd recognized that sooner. It wasn't too late.

He walked away

"What are you doing? Come back here."

Nope. Let Ellona have her temper tantrum alone. Someone else could deal with her.

"You can't just leave. You owe me. Bastard."

The nearness of the last hissed word made him whirl. "My parents were very much mated."

She glowered from less than a pace away. "You're just making it easy for me, aren't you? You really shouldn't have come."

"You're right. I shouldn't have." As he shook his

head, she swiped, the fingers tipped in claws a nasty surprise.

He retreated a step as Ellona spawned into a hybrid shape, still two legged, but wearing scaled armor. It layered her skin, hooded her eyes. Her exterior now impenetrable to regular metal, even dragon teeth and claws. It would also repel most magic. Only a weapon forged of dracinore could hurt her.

And he was fresh out of any.

"You'd really kill me?" He didn't particularly like Ellona, but that didn't mean he'd murder her.

"A thousand times if I could." A cold smile tugged her armored lips.

"Still with the violence and threats? This is a new world, Ellona. A new chance for us all."

"All but you." She flicked her wrist, and a blade shot from her hand, long and wickedly sharp. She eyed it then him. Her grin quite wicked. "Ask me how many times I fantasized about impaling you on my sword."

Before he could conjure something in response, someone shouted, "Don't kill him."

Maalik could have groaned as he realized who'd come to his rescue. He half turned and snapped, "What are you doing? I told you to stay out of sight."

"I was, until people ran past the restaurant screaming. I thought you might need my help." Daava sounded sincere, and her expression matched. She was dressed in mismatched clothes, shapeless and yet so beautiful.

He softened. "This isn't a good time."

Creak. Ellona intentionally rubbed her scales as she asked icily, "Who is this?"

"No one," he muttered.

"I'm Daava."

He wanted to groan.

"You seem familiar," Ellona stated with a sniff.

"Really? Because I don't think we've met," Daava replied.

A good thing because if Ellona guessed who she spoke with…

He had to separate them. "Go wait for me by the sweets shops. I'll handle this." He inclined his head.

"No, let her stay. I'm curious. There's something odd about you, Daava," Ellona purred. "A stench of magic and a reminder of home. But you're not a dragon."

"Leave her out of this," Maalik warned.

"Why? Is she important to you? Because if she is, I'm confused. Didn't you come here to try and beg me to love you again?"

Shame almost burned his cheeks. Almost. Instead, he let the searing heat of anger at his own stupidity be his guide. "I came to see how you were. Nothing more."

"I'm angry. What are you going to do to fix it?"

"Nothing. I'm not taking the blame for what happened. I told you I didn't want you coming. You insisted. What was I supposed to do?"

"I only insisted because I thought you were trying to shut me out of the glory. Or did you think I didn't notice how you basked in the attention as people commended you for saving them?"

"What are you talking about? All of us received special attention because we all fought."

"Me harder than the others," she spat. "I was the one who usually managed to shred the Shaitan, breaking them down so we could rest and recuperate before they gathered themselves again."

"You did make quite the name for yourself," Daava agreed.

Ellona's attention shifted. "How would you know?"

"Because I told her stories." Maalik hastily jumped in to try and divert the conversation.

It failed. Ellona's gaze narrowed. "We've already ascertained you're not dragon. And despite the body, not human. What are you? Because I know that scent. Spicy and smoky."

"It's not important," Maalik said, too late.

The blade at the end of Ellona's arm thrust, penetrating Daava's chest to a hissed, "Shaitan!"

Chapter Twenty-One

The first surprise?

A sword shoved into flesh hurt.

The second?

The amount of blood that began to spill the moment the blade retreated. How could she be bleeding?

Daava fell to the ground and gaped at the sky. Her lips bubbled, frothing with fluid as she struggled to breathe.

Magic. She needed power to fix the wound, only her thoughts scattered. She couldn't hold the threads of it long enough before the pain scattered it.

Maalik dropped to his knees and peered at her. "Heal yourself."

Her lips moved, but nothing emerged. If only

she could focus. It reminded her of being at the bottom of the lake, knowing she had the magic to help herself, just unable to access it.

Concern creased his brow. "Daava? Don't you dare die." He sounded genuinely worried.

So was she. Because it appeared her flesh could be damaged, and if she couldn't repair it, what happened if the body ceased to live?

"Why do you care if the Shaitan dies?" Ellona screeched, piercing enough that Daava winced.

"I care because…" He glanced down. "Because it is possible to change. To admit you might have been wrong. To start over." He reached out and stroked Daava's hair, his touch gentle, his expression soft. "Never too late to admit I was wrong. It's my fault she's here and got injured. I can fix this. I wish for the Daava I am touching to heal her wound."

The gasp that left Daava's lips didn't entirely escape because of the bargain that focused her magic and immediately acted to heal. A greater shock filled her than the burn of magic.

He used a wish to save me.

No one had ever done that before. No one had cared when they hurt her. She couldn't die. She was a Jinn. Her pain didn't matter.

To anyone but Maalik.

He saved her from finding out if she could die.

Compelled to act, her magic funneled into her and then through her, repairing the damage left by the sword and making her whole. She sat up and pressed a hand to her chest.

"Are you healed?" he asked.

She nodded, pleased by his concern.

He should have been more worried about the woman at his back.

"You wasted a wish on *it*?"

Maalik rose from his haunches and turned to face Ellona. "I did."

"You saved a Shaitan?"

"You say that like it's a foul word. Yet what do we really know about them?" Maalik stood protectively in front of her.

"They're evil," Ellona stated as if it were fact.

Daava peeked around Maalik's legs and argued, "It's not evil to want to survive."

"Of course, you'd claim some kind of pity story. Poor Shaitan, so abused," Ellona taunted.

"Are you done with your childish tactics? Perhaps we should try listening to each other for once," Maalik stated.

"Listening? Is that what you're doing when you're fucking her?" A cruel sneer tugged Ellona's features.

Daava studied the other woman, who appeared

the opposite of her. Slender where she was curvy, her features stark and sharp, her hair short and wispy.

"Daava and I aren't lovers," Maalik corrected. "*Yet*," he emphasized. "I'm hoping that will change."

The admission stunned Daava.

"You always were easily led by your cock," Ellona mocked. "Were you hoping that by fucking her you would receive more wishes?"

"That's not how wishes work, and you know it."

"I do know, which is why I am wondering how many wishes you have left. Because you wasted one healing her. Was that your first? Second? Last? Can't be last, or why would she still be around?" Ellona mused aloud.

"Daava is none of your business."

"Oh, but she is. Because if you've run out of wishes, then that means she's available to be captured and freed."

Daava couldn't help herself. "I'd rather you didn't."

"More like you can't." Maalik crossed his arms. "Daava has yet to fulfill her bargain to me."

It confused her that he appeared loath to speak of his last wish. Hadn't he spoken of giving it to Ellona? It appeared he'd changed his mind.

"The way I see it, we have two choices." Ellona ticked a finger. "You die and I get three wishes, or you give me your remaining one or two, whatever you have left. After all, you owe me."

He grimaced. "You're not the only one."

"And yet I'm the one who will kill you if you try and walk away."

"Now, now. Is that any way to talk to the man you were supposed to wed?" a new voice drawled.

The fellow from the forge suddenly appeared on a slow-moving horse, the size and breadth daunting. Upon his shoulder perched a cat, who regarded them all with a bored eye.

"This doesn't concern you, Isafril." Ellona turned her attention from Daava.

"Actually, it does, because you're being an idiot. You both are. Do you realize what kind of spectacle you've caused?" Israfil swept a gauntlet-covered hand. "There are bodies."

"I told them to move," Maalik argued.

"They're just humans," was Ellona's excuse.

"Are you trying to start a war with them?" Israfil spoke quietly but firmly. "Maalik, I expected better of you. Then again you've always been an idiot where she is concerned." He sneered in Ellona's direction. Then Israfil turned his gaze on Daava. "There you are. I've been looking for you."

A chill went through Daava at the sight of the stave that apparated into his hand. *The God Killer.* The weapon that could supposedly kill Jinn.

"You aren't destroying her," Maalik declared.

"Do it!" Ellona exclaimed with too much glee. "Stab the Shaitan whore in front of her lover. It might be worth losing wishes to see Maalik writhing in pain."

All this talk of killing Daava, especially since she still shook from her recent almost-death experience, had her slowly retreating.

Perhaps she should have listened to Maalik and remained hidden. Yet, when she'd heard the metal dragon was attacking a man, she'd panicked. She'd had no thought but to ensure his safety.

And now, he tried to bargain for hers.

Because he cared.

No, he doesn't.

The insidious whisper wrapped around her.

He saved me using one of his wishes.

Because if he hadn't, he'd have none.

No. That's not true. He cares for me.

No, he doesn't. The internal argument continued. *He's only ever wanted to reunite with his true love.*

That's not love. At least not how she imagined it.

Love is not real.

The remark jarred her enough that she blinked.

Of course, love was real. It was the one constant among the flesh-wearing. They cared. She cared.

Jinn don't love.

I do. It was then she realized she'd not been internally debating herself. *Get out of my head.*

She shoved at the thoughts touching hers, so similar, so very familiar she'd not felt them creeping.

The Jinn who'd attempted to merge with her mind appeared, a dark fog that remained shapeless as it hung before her.

They have infected the spirit. Wisps of it reached for her flesh.

"Don't touch me." She shifted and tried to remain out of reach.

Failed. The smoky Jinn wrapped itself in dark bands that bound her.

"What do they want?" she asked.

Time to rejoin the collective.

"I don't want to."

There is no I. Only the mission.

"I don't wish to be a part of that plan."

There is no choice.

"Actually, I do get to choose because this is my life." She glanced at Maalik. A man who'd inadvertently taught her all about it.

The mage does not care.

"He does." She only had to recall how he'd used

his wish. How she incited him to the point his stabbing tool was always at the ready around her.

Hear the truth.

Voices suddenly projected, Maalik, Ellona, and Israfil, arguing as if they stood close.

"Out of my way, Maal. This is going to happen." A gruff demand by Israfil.

"You are not killing her."

"Why are you fighting me on this? You know how dangerous the Shaitan are. It must be eliminated before it can cause problems."

"Her name is Daava."

"I don't give a fuck what her name is," Israfil stated. "And if this is about the wishes she owes you, too bad. You should have used them up. At least you managed the main one. Ellona's alive."

"You wished for me to live?" The surprise was clear in Ellona's tone.

"Turns out I didn't need to," Maalik grumbled. "Still can't believe you faked your death."

"Only because I was angry at the time." Ellona batted her lashes. "I regretted it right away, but by then, it was too late. I couldn't find my way back to you. But I'm here now. Let's forget all this ugliness. We'll use up your last wish, and then you'll help me capture the Shaitan so that we can free it for more wishes."

"No." He said it firmly.

"I'm going to echo Maalik here," Israfil butted in. "No more wishing. It's caused nothing but trouble."

"Stay out of this. This is between me and Maalik," Ellona snarled. "He owes me."

Maalik hung his head. "How many times can I say I'm sorry, Ellona? I'd do anything for you—"

Whatever else he said was lost as the conversation cut off.

But Daava had heard enough. It would seem whatever she thought Maalik might feel paled in comparison to his love for Ellona.

Tears for a dragon mage? They managed repulsion. They didn't understand what it was like to feel. Perhaps that was a boon given the sickness filling her.

Enough of the emotions. It is time. The collective awaits.

Sadness didn't mean she intended to give in. "No. I'm not—" *Gag. Choke.* Her eyes widened as a tendril of mist entered through her mouth. She couldn't spit out. It wiggled its way inside, bringing panic and discomfort.

And then she felt nothing. Nothing at all.

Chapter Twenty-Two

The argument went round in circles, and the longer it did, the more it disgusted Maalik. Israfil clung staunchly to his insistence that all Shaitan should die. Ellona persisted her greed in not wanting only one wish but demanding he trap Daava and enslave her for even more.

Never.

The avarice in Ellona's gaze let him know she wouldn't settle for one, let alone four wishes. Who knew what cruelty she'd demand? After all, she'd already expressed an extreme dislike for the ruling humans. It wasn't a stretch to believe she'd wish a plague on them, or worse.

He still remembered a story told to him by his grandfather about a man named Noah who happened to release a Jinn from a lamp, meaning he got three wishes. Noah hated his neighbors, so he wished for a boat and then wished for two of every animal in the world. Then the last wish…a flood. Which, unfortunately, killed Noah as he was trying to convince two unicorns that had fled to return aboard.

The exhausted Jinn fled and was never heard of again. As for Noah's ark? The flood occurred only in Noah's valley. and when the waters receded, the boat was found. Noah's family was dead. Actually most of the ship's occupants had died to feed the large cats on board.

He had no doubt Ellona would cause something just as catastrophic, perhaps even more violent given her temper. He couldn't allow that to happen. However, the simple solution of letting Israfil eliminate Daava wasn't an option either.

"Both of you need to stop talking about Daava as if she is a thing. She's a person with thoughts and feelings."

"Listen, Maal"—Israfil grabbed him by the shoulders for a little shake—"I know she looks normal, but she's still Jinn inside."

"It's more than looks. She feels. Daava can bleed, Israfil."

"She did and copiously. It was quite sickening to watch Maalik fawn over her as if it were fatal."

Ellona's moue of distaste had him turning away in disgust.

He searched for Daava and found her leaning against the base of the tower wreathed in a fog.

She wasn't alone.

"Israfil, keep your stave handy. It appears we have company," Maalik said.

As all eyes turned to Daava, she pushed off the wall and strode toward them, the misty Shaitan a shadow alongside. How long had it been there? Had it harmed Daava? She didn't appear to be in any distress. She didn't appear to have any expression at all.

As she neared, the blankness only became more blatant. Her eyes were just dark pools with no nuance. No humor.

No life...

"Daava?" He felt stupid saying her name aloud, and yet looking upon her, he'd have sworn she was someone else.

"Can I help you, Master?" No inflection or even a hint of mockery.

"Are you okay? Did that Shaitan harm you?"

"They are fine, Master."

He noticed the choice in pronoun. "They? What happened to 'me'? What happened to you not wanting to be part of the Jinn collective?"

"They have seen the error of their ways."

"Sounds like your Shaitan whore has betrayed you." Ellona uttered an ugly chuckle.

"They're controlling her somehow. I know she's in there. Daava?"

No recognition in her eyes at all.

It hurt him because this was his fault. He'd brought her here. He'd caused her to be caught.

"Maal, watch out." Israfil shoved at him before Ellona charged past. Her bladed hand swung, and the smoky Shaitan dispersed before it connected, but Daava didn't move. Lip pulled back in a snarl, Ellona thrust again and hit an invisible shield protecting Daava.

The smoky Shaitan reappeared.

"My turn," Israfil said flatly, and yet his response was fiery. Balls of pure fire appeared midair and rolled, gathering speed as they aimed for the shadowy shape. The Shaitan dissolved before contact and the fireballs slammed into the ground. That didn't stop Israfil from launching more, keeping the Shaitan occupied while his cat remained on his shoulders, claws dug in, and hissing.

The spell preventing Maalik from shifting remained annoyingly in place, but the same restriction didn't appear to impact his magic. He went after the Shaitan because it had to have done something to Daava. Perhaps if they distracted it, or incapacitated it, whatever spell it had placed upon her would disappear.

Only the Shaitan remained as slippery to catch as ever, vanishing as smoke, then reappearing elsewhere, solid only long enough to launch an attack. Israfil did his best to dance and predict the next move, However, the fight between Ellona and Daava led to a few stumbles.

Sirens wailed in the distance. The humans had sent their armed soldiers. This had to end.

Only one idea came to mind.

He ran for Daava and spread his arms wide.

The blank expression on her face speared him but didn't dissuade him from shoving her hard with a magical push of wind. Right into a portal.

He jumped in after her.

Chapter Twenty-Three

The sudden change of scenery didn't cease the Shaitan's barrage of fire. Upon stabilizing on the other side, they whirled and kept flinging ball after ball of flame.

To no avail.

The dragon mage stood defiantly in front of them, a magical shield deflecting every single attempt to destroy him. The mage spoke, trying to address a singular that no longer existed.

They were the collective. The sum of all Jinn. The servants of the Iblis who would find a new way to return their master that it might free them from the whims of those with flesh. The Iblis would kill the Jinn enemy. Like the mage in front of them. The one who'd locked them away.

"Daava, if you're in there, give me a sign," he

begged. He'd yet to retaliate. On the contrary, he'd been protecting them even from his ally with the fearful stave.

"Just give up and die," they said, bored of the impasse, as yet another attack spattered aside with no damage.

"I'm not giving up on you. I know this isn't what you want."

"There is no want. We serve the Iblis."

"Ever think of just serving yourself?"

"There is only us. We are serving us," they hissed.

"No, you're serving the Iblis."

"Enough." Arguing served no purpose but wasting time. They should leave. They'd still more to gather before the Jinn collective was complete.

They didn't move. Nor could they smoke, as they remained caught solidly in flesh.

Strange. They flexed fingers and took notice of the body.

"You have to fight, Daava. Remember what it's like to be you."

They remembered everything. From their arrival after the bargain, an explosion of motes that were naturally drawn to each other, sharing a multitude of experiences. Some of them censored for being disturbing.

Individuality should never be condoned.

I like being me.

They have no need of like, only duty.

Duty to someone else? There was laughter in their thoughts. It wasn't theirs, and it refused to stay quiet. *You can't keep me tucked in here forever. I will find a way out.*

They tried to ignore it.

I know you can hear me. Give me back my body.

Their body, actually.

Mine. Give. It. Back.

Daava struggled to ride past the blanketing nature of the Jinn collective. The piece that infiltrated her was new and hadn't gone through the same metamorphosis she had while in the ring.

Daava had found the solitude peaceful. Enlightening. Quiet.

They feared being cut off. Never wanted to feel as if they were alone again.

But Daava missed it, so she fought back.

This is my body.

Not some kind of tool they could use to bring back the Iblis. Who cared about the Iblis?

I am not helping. The Ibis needs to stay where it is.

They will do as told.

Wrong.

Daava wasn't just one part of the whole. Daava

was all of it. Every single Jinn piece that formed her belonged to her, and the one that had snuck inside? Easy to track down once she made the choice and expunged it.

The tiny wisp, barely enough to merit the name Jinn, hovered before her. It would take her back over if given a chance.

Maalik reacted swiftly. A flask appeared suddenly in his hand, and he chanted. The air cracked and then whistled as the neck of the bottle began to suck. The tiny piece of Jinn she'd expelled didn't stand a chance.

Only once he stoppered it did Daava blink at him and say, "I am glad I didn't kill you."

Chapter Twenty-Four

As Daava returned to herself, Maalik heaved a sigh of relief that he choked on as she added, "I don't think it's considered appropriate to kiss dead people."

"No, it's not. Is it really you?"

Her lips quirked. "Me. Myself. And I."

"I'm glad. What happened?"

"The collective. They tried to infiltrate."

"You managed to rid yourself of it." He couldn't help but be impressed. "How did you break free?"

"It wasn't a part of me. Never would be. Because I am me. And I'd like to stay that way."

He smiled. "I'm proud of you."

"Are you?" she teased. "Do I get a prize?"

"What would you like?" Please let it be what he

thought he read in her gaze. She offered him a sultry smile. The practical mage reminded him that they were still in peril, but that would require someone tracking them down. Unlikely, and besides, he had wards.

"I am thinking another lesson in touching." She put her hand on his chest.

He almost died. No, he couldn't, because he wanted what would happen next. "I don't know if I can keep it to just touching this time."

"Will there be stabbing, too?" She grinned.

"I hope so," he growled, dragging her into his arms. Only he paused before kissing her. "You're not saying yes to sex because of that last wish, are you? This isn't me commanding you."

She chuckled. "I know. This is something I want."

"Just making sure you felt free to choose."

Wrong choice of words. She stiffened before softly saying, "What's it like to be free?"

The questioned startled, and it took him a moment to form a reply. "I'm not sure I know." He hastened to explain. "You're bound by a promise made a long time ago, and I'm a peon to the futures I see, trying to make things better, but oftentimes only making it worse."

"What happens when you don't see the future?"

"I'm lost. I have to muddle along like a mere mortal, making choices and not knowing if they're the right ones. What's it like to be Jinn?"

"It's..." She hesitated. "Different. When I was incorporeal, my goals were different because I thought differently. But in this body..." She wiggled against him. "It's about feeling good. Physically but also mentally. There is enjoyment in both."

"And what physical things do you enjoy?" he asked, his gaze intent.

She boldly met it. "Eating, for one."

"Eating? What about when I kiss you?"

"It's nice."

"Only nice?" he teased, the words brushing her lips.

Her breath hitched. "Perhaps I need a reminder."

He couldn't have said which one exhaled first as they embraced. He only knew their lips melded, their tongues sliding and his blood boiling hard enough he might explode. Some of their clothes disappeared as they ended up on the bed, kissing with hands exploring. He'd never felt happier.

And exposed as a chilly Ellona growled, "Isn't this touching."

Passion swapped to alertness. Maalik rolled off Daava and, with magic, redressed himself quickly before he faced off against Ellona. "How did you find us?"

"Would you like me to spout some platitude about my jealousy suddenly exposing my undying love for you that led to me having the power to track you down?"

"That's not a thing anyone can do," Daava declared, standing by his side wearing only a shirt.

"Be quiet. No one was speaking to you."

He sighed. "What do you want, Ellona?"

"You owe me."

"I told you, I don't. Not my fault you regret your actions."

"I want your last wish." She stamped her foot stubbornly.

"Which is exactly why you're not getting it."

Only one person deserved a wish. And by getting rid of it, hopefully he'd be done with Ellona, too.

Chapter Twenty-Five

Just as Daava was debating where to place the penis on Ellona's face, Maalik said the most impossible thing.

"I wish the one I know as Daava to be free from the Jinn curse."

What?

She had to have misheard. What was he doing? Any doubt she might have had vanished as the bargain took over. The last wish had been invoked, and it was a big one.

It started with a tingle in her toes then the tips of her fingers. The tingling intensified, and she felt as if she inflated and thinned out all at once. She felt light, yet immense. Hungry, too. Her entire being hummed as something in her shifted.

The humming line within her suddenly snapped and didn't return. She knew what it meant.

She no longer had to follow the rules of the bargain because Maalik had used his last wish to free her. In doing so, he ensured she would never be beholden to anyone again. The idea terrified and excited.

"Daava, are you okay?"

She opened her eyes to find Maalik kneeling beside her. "What did you do?

His lips quirked. "Used my wish for good. I think."

"I'm not a Jinn anymore."

"Ending your curse was the only way I could think of to help you." He appeared worried, as if he might have done the wrong thing.

She grinned. "No more wishes. And I have a body." She'd kept the one she was in.

"Are you okay with that?"

"It's what I've wanted for a long time."

He held out his hand. "Can you stand?"

She reached for his fingers, and he hauled her to her feet then reeled her close enough for a hug. There might have been a kiss, too, if Ellona hadn't once more interrupted.

"What did you do?" the shrill woman railed.

"I used my wish," Maalik stated quite smugly.

"But I wanted it," Ellona whined, getting close enough to jab Maalik in the chest with her finger.

Daava didn't like it one bit. "Oh, stop it with the guilt. As a person who is well versed when it comes to debt, I can state with assurance he owes you nothing."

"Shut your trap. I sliced you open once, I will slice you again," Ellona threatened.

The challenge brought a smile. "Try it. I don't think you'll find it as easy this time." Because within she felt a new power.

"I am going to rip you apart, limb by limb," Ellona growled.

A bugle overhead drew their gazes to a spiraling silver dragon with a rider on its back. It swooped in for a landing.

"Girl fight. I want a front row seat," Babette declared the moment she shifted.

Ellona's attention was on Jeebrelle. "You!"

"Hello, Ellona. I see you unfortunately managed to find your way out."

"No thanks to you," Ellona spat.

"I told you, I had no idea where he put the amulet," Jeebrelle stated.

"And even if he had, you wouldn't have told me," Ellona spat.

"You're right. I wouldn't have because, while I

didn't like it, I respected the oath I made," Jeebrelle retorted. "Whereas you ran off like a spoiled dragonling. Made us all think you were dead.

"To get away from him." Ellona glared at Maalik.

"Don't be blaming anyone but yourself. I offered you a place to stay if you didn't want to be a couple anymore. You chose to pretend you died instead. And then, tried to start a war with the humans." Jeebrelle turned to Maalik. "I don't suppose you can put her back where the wish found her."

"Afraid there's no more wishes."

"Pity. It would have been simplest given she caused quite the ruckus," Jeebrelle chided. "The humans are in an uproar."

A hair toss went with Ellona's, "And?"

"And we're gonna have to take you in for judging by the king," Babette drawled. "Then, unless we've managed to scrub the many videos and plant a story to cover why a bunch of people died horrifically and shit burned down, we'll probably have to hand you over to human authorities for judgment."

"The humans don't rule me. No one here will tell me what to do." Ellona whirled and slashed fast enough that there was no dodging the strike.

But Daava expected perfidy. That strangeness inside shifted, and Daava was suddenly a dragon with a carapace hard enough to block the blow. With a mighty paw, she flattened the annoying mage and held her pinned on the ground.

I'm a dragon.

And not just any dragon.

Babette exclaimed, "Holy fuck, she's a ginormous Pink Pearl Unicorn Dragon!"

Chapter Twenty-Six

Once Babette got over her excitement, a magic-bound Ellona was taken away for judgment. If deemed worthy, she might escape death and be offered rehabilitation.

Their departure left Maalik alone with Daava, a free woman.

And a dragon.

She seemed quite pleased by that fact. "I wonder why the magic chose dragon."

"Dragon mage I would wager given the horn."

"Babette says I am a rare beauty." She clasped her hands.

"You always were. How's it feel to know you don't have to grant any more wishes? You'll only make your own choices from now on."

"It's…freeing." She beamed.

"What are you going to do first?"

Her lips curved in mischief. "How about finally get that stabbing you've been teasing me about?"

"Uh…" He, the greatest dragon mage seer of his time, speechless because he'd not seen Daava coming and now couldn't imagine a future without her. But did she feel the same?

"Nothing to say?" She stepped closer. "What if I say I want to be with you?"

"Are you sure? Because you could have anyone you wanted," he stupidly stated, but he had to be sure she understood she didn't have to settle.

"I don't want anyone but you." She leaned close to breathe hotly on his lips. "Are you going to keep arguing or show me pleasure?"

"Your wish is my command."

Their lips met in a fiery clash of lips and teeth. The passion was explosive. Her hands tore at him as eagerly as he stripped her.

A combination of magics floated their clinging, naked bodies to the mattress that, by now, needed replacing. They never once lost the lock of their lips. Her body undulated against his, a sinuous delight.

Everything he did was met with a gasp of pleasure. He kissed her neck, she moaned. He sucked a pert nipple and she gasped. A hand between her legs had her squirming.

She was wet. Perfectly so. And he was tempted to just sink deep.

First, though, he dropped between her thighs and licked. He licked her until she grabbed the sheets on their borrowed bed and arched from it. He flicked his tongue until she keened and thrashed. Even as her orgasm still gripped her, his tongue kept working her, as did the finger he slid inside.

He licked and thrust until her hips were rocking again, only then did he cover her with his body. His lips met hers, and he whispered, "Are you sure?"

"My body, my choice. Stab me," she demanded.

He eased into her, her tightness making him rigid and slow. She quivered around him, and he was almost undone.

She stiffened, and he prepared to withdraw, thinking perhaps she'd changed her mind.

Her lips caught his as she said, "I think I am going to orgasm again."

He almost did at her words. He controlled himself enough to start thrusting deep enough that he caught her sweet spot and had her rocking in time. Their bodies moved as one. Their pleasure crashed into and with each other.

Being inside her as she came proved a pleasure like no other. And he stayed inside her even as their tempos slowed and their passion cooled.

He leaned his forehead against hers. "That was incredible."

"Will it always be like that?" she asked.

"Yes." Because he and Daava didn't just have sex. They made love—

To an audience that said, "Think they're done, or is he going right away for round two?"

Epilogue

After the incident in Toronto, videos of which were widely spread on the internet, plus the interruption in their field by curiosity seekers looking for the unidragon, Daava and Maalik disappeared from the public and dragon eye. They had no interest in serving the world. Not anymore. The time to be a little selfish had arrived.

They built a house by a different lake in another hidden valley. Supplies were brought in by magic, but they used their hands and tools to put it together. They only resorted to using their power for the parts that required a more skilled touch.

By the time they finished, they had a home, not a palace, featuring a giant bed, a bathroom with a tub large enough for two, and a kitchen with a pantry and fridge both big enough to walk in—kept fully stocked, of course, and replenished as quickly as it was emptied. Daava enjoyed food too much to hoard it. For her special stash, she'd discovered a keen love of all things Unikitty—Blame Babette who introduced her to the character—and had begun a collection.

It wasn't the only thing she owned.

The biggest television with all the possible channels hung on a wall. Another wall held books, shelves and shelves of them. Although Maalik did glance askance at her bare-chested favorites. Romance didn't just happen in real life, but in books! She couldn't read enough of them, and Maalik learned to not mock given he reaped the reward when she pounced, intent on ravishing his body.

If she'd expected an adjustment to being a mortal with flesh, she'd thought wrong. There was nothing to miss. As a Jinn, and then Shaitan, she'd never been free. Never known anything but strife.

Now she had love. The kind of love she read about in stories. The kind that made her tingle and smile.

A love so perfect it performed the greatest magic of all.

Her palm rested on her stomach.

Standing at her back, his hand pressed over

hers, Maalik leaned to whisper in her ear, "Our child will do great things."

Maybe one day even rule the world, she thought with a smile.

JEEBRELLE MET Babette in their usual spot.

Did she notice Babette used a new conditioner that left her hair softer and curlier than usual? Babette sure as hell admired the slim-fitting trousers that showed off Jeebs's lithe limbs.

"Any luck finding Maalik and the little genie?"

Who was a genie no longer since Maalik's last wish. But the authorities didn't care. Daava had caused quite a bit of damage during her fiery rampage and, given the antics of the other Shaitan, drawn the attention of humanity. The hunt was on to find the Jinn which unfortunately also focused attention on the dragons.

"Maalik can't hide forever," Jeebs grumbled.

"What of Ellona?" The metal dragon had disappeared as well, which was a cause for concern given images from the scene at the CN Tower showed the woman wearing an amulet. An amulet that Jeebrelle was convinced held a Shaitan inside.

"I don't know. But you can bet we haven't seen

the last of her. I warned Maalik she wasn't stable enough to endure our time in stasis."

"Love can make a person do crazy things." Like make Babette tongue-tied around a certain pale rider.

"Speaking of crazy, in speaking with my brethren, we've come to believe the danger posed by the Iblis isn't over. The Shaitan appear to have a new plan. It is imperative we locate the remaining seals before they do. Would you be interested in helping?"

Babette immediately volunteered and was more than delighted when Jeebs added, "We make a good team."

"That we do."

"You'll soon be part of an even more epic one," Elspeth announced, suddenly joining them.

"What have you seen, prophetess?" Jeebrelle had great respect for Elspeth.

"Soon you'll be flying on a most important mission. It will be glorious if the drunken eagle can find his iron mettle again," Elspeth added with a cryptic smile.

Babette had only one further question. "Will it be dangerous?"

"Very."

"I'm in."

Jeebrelle placed her hand over Babette's and said, "We're both in."

Swoon.

FROM A HIDDEN SPOT perched atop his servant's shoulders, the cat watched as the silver dragon flew off, a pale rider on her back.

Wasting their time. The feline sniffed. As if their actions would make a difference. What would come, would come. Not that the humans or even dragons would listen. Always with the drama.

Much better to be a cat.

Especially when its human chose to scratch behind the ears.

So many exciting things still to happen! Next in Dragon Point, we have Dragon's Kitty *featuring Israfil and his mysterious pet. But before that story, get ready to jump back into Kodiak Point and embark on a mini mission with dragons when a former soldier seeks redemption in* Iron Eagle.

www.ingramcontent.com/pod-product-compliance
Lightning Source LLC
LaVergne TN
LVHW041629060526
838200LV00040B/1508